EAGLE E.Y.E.

E.Y.E. Spy Mystery #2

CHERYL KAYE TARDIF

EAGLE E.Y.E.
E.Y.E. Spy Mystery #2

http://www.cherylktardif.com

FIRST EDITION Trade Paperback

December 12, 2017

Published by Imajin Qwickies®, an imprint of Imajin Books®

http://www.ImajinQwickies.com

ISBN: 978-1-77223-315-5

Cover design by Ryan Doan: http://www.ryandoan.com

Chapter One

A tooth lay in the palm of Eileen Edwards' hand, a thin streak of near-black indicating dried blood near the root. No big deal on its own. However, the larger evidence bag sitting on her kitchen island gave Eileen cause for concern. The bag contained blood-covered leaves and twigs.

"Someone is in a world of hurt," she said. "Human molar, I presume?"

Constable Larry Norman gave a grim nod. He'd been her partner, back when she'd worn the uniform. "Lab says it's from a female between thirty and forty years old, but there's no DNA match in our system. Report shows enough ketamine in her blood to knock out a horse."

"When and where was this discovered?"

"Two days ago. In the back woods near Eagle Ridge Golf & Country Club. A twelve-year-old boy found the tooth and blood while searching for golf balls."

"Poor kid." Eileen deposited the tooth in a small, clear bag and set it on the granite counter. "And you're heading this case?"

"Rick Martin is. But the department is stretched to the limits of our resources, so I told him I'd ask for your help, since you're one of us."

"*Was* one of you, you mean. Why couldn't Martin ask me himself?"

Larry shrugged. "I think he's intimidated by you."

"What?"

"Your reputation for being a ballbuster precedes you." He chuckled. "Rick Martin and Luis Cayolla are working this case."

"Cayolla?" She frowned. "Isn't he the one who's a stickler for following protocol to the letter?"

"He's a good guy, just not used to big-city crimes—or our pace."

Eileen refilled Larry's coffee mug. "What does Martin want me to do?"

"While he and Cayolla visit hospitals

and medi-centers to see if a bleeding, drugged woman with a missing molar has been admitted, they'd like you to check out the Eagle Ridge connection."

Eileen scrutinized the blood-soaked flora in the bag. "That's a lot of blood for a tooth."

"And there's more at the scene." Larry reached into his briefcase. "One of our guys also found *this*." He held up a third evidence bag. "Woman's scarf, silk, traces of DNA, but again, no match to anyone in the system. Whoever this woman is, she's never been convicted of a crime. No fingerprints, no DNA samples on file. However, the blood on the scarf does match DNA from the scene."

She took a photo of the scarf with the new smartphone acquired when she'd bought Zoe's cell phone. "So same victim."

Larry nodded. "Somehow, a woman was drugged, either before or after arriving at Eagle Ridge, and then able to get past security cameras before losing a lot of blood and a tooth in the woods. Not your normal round of golf."

"May I?" She picked up the bag, noting that the royal blue and aqua-colored scarf wasn't a cheap Walmart bargain but probably imported from India. Someone had removed the tag. She took a close-up photo of the scarf pattern. A warm waft of sandalwood teased her nostrils, and she sniffed the bag. "Perfume. The real stuff. Not one of those watered-down knockoffs."

"The lab identified it as *Joy*."

"That's kind of ironic."

"It's a French perfume made by..." Larry consulted his cell phone. "Ah, here it is...made by Jean Patou."

"Sounds expensive."

"It's only eight hundred dollars an ounce—American."

Eileen whistled. "I'll stick to Vanilla Fields."

"Now you know why we need you."

"I was supposed to take Zoe to the Pacific National Exhibition today, since she's on summer holidays." Gritting her teeth, she released a slow hiss of air. "Do you have any idea what the rest of my day will be like if I piss off a teenager promised a day at the PNE?"

Her former partner shrugged. "Zipper—I mean, Zoe—has a sharp eye. Maybe your foster daughter can help with the computer stuff." He handed her three manila folders. "Martin would like you to go through these missing persons reports and search for any connection to the golf course. The second folder is the membership list for Eagle Ridge. The last one includes all guests who have registered at the club over the past year."

"You know, the department has techies for this kind of work."

"The higher-ups want a private investigator on the case, someone who'd be less conspicuous than a uniform. I suggested you."

"Why so cautious?"

"Eagle Ridge is worried about their stellar reputation."

"And so they should. A hole-in-one shouldn't include blood and teeth."

"So you'll do it?"

Eileen sighed. "You can count me in."

"I never doubted that for a second," Larry said with a grin. "I'll let Martin and Cayolla know."

"Your timing sucks."

"Thank you, Eileen. And thank Zoe for me. I'll owe her."

Eileen cocked a brow at him. "Believe me, Zoe will collect."

After Larry left, she filled her mug with Chai tea and headed to work.

Several months after she'd left the police force, Eileen had converted one of three garages into a roomy office for her *E.Y.E. Spy Investigations* business. In between cases of philandering spouses, deadbeat dads or runaway teens, she consulted on cases with Vancouver Police. That's how she'd inherited Zoe and Alfie, her new housemates.

Eileen's home office presented a state of chaotic disarray. Stacks of folders and documents lay on almost every flat surface that wasn't covered by a computer, printer or stereo system. While not the neatest person on the planet, Eileen prided herself on knowing exactly where everything was— kind of like J.K. Rowling.

She cleared off the wooden desk by the window and set the missing persons reports next to her laptop. "Now for the tough part." Telling Zoe she wouldn't be eating cotton candy or riding rollercoasters until she puked.

"Who are you talking to?"

Eileen let out a startled gasp. "Jesus, Zoe! Don't sneak up on me like that."

Her foster daughter smiled. "You always talk to yourself like that?"

"Some days more than others, kiddo.

You should know that by now."

The girl standing before her was small but lean for her age. Thick, dark brown hair hung past her shoulders, with a few wisps of sun-kissed blonde framing her pretty face. She looked nothing like the "Zipper kid" Eileen had been hired to find months ago when Zoe had hidden behind a boy's identity to escape abuse on the streets. Lord knows what the poor girl had witnessed, other than that gang hit. That was bad enough.

"I need to talk to you for a minute," Eileen began. "About our plans."

Zoe's bright blue eyes faded with disappointment. "We're not going to the PNE, are we?"

"I'm sorry. Constable Norman stopped by this morning to ask me for help with a case."

The girl scowled. "But this is supposed to be *our* day."

"I know, and I'm really sorry about this." Eileen pointed to the stack of papers on the table. "I have to go through all those reports. I could use some help, if you're game."

Excitement flashed in Zoe's eyes. "Really? I get to work on a case with you?"

She plopped into the chair and started rifling through the reports.

"Whoa! You don't even know what you're looking for yet."

"What's the case?"

Oh God, how to describe this one in kid terms…

Eileen took a deep breath and told Zoe about the gruesome discovery at Eagle Ridge. The kid had seen worse.

"We need to look for any connections between the women in this pile and Eagle Ridge Golf & Country Club."

"I finished da laundry, Miss Eileen," a voice sang from the doorway.

"Alfie should help too," Zoe said.

The black woman in the doorway plodded into the room. "Sure. I got nothin' to do now 'til supper."

Alfie had come to live with Eileen at the same time as Zoe. The woman claimed to be seventy-one, much older than Eileen's forty-nine years, and she'd lived on the streets and befriended Zoe back when the girl called herself "Zipper." Alfie had a few OCD tendencies, which worked in Eileen's favor. Her home—with the exception of Eileen's office—had never looked cleaner. More importantly, the woman could cook.

Zoe flipped open the laptop. "You give me their names, Eileen, and I'll search online for info on them. And Alfie can compare names to Eagle Ridge's members and take notes."

"Alrighty, boss-girl," Eileen said. "Let's get to work."

By the time they were finished, the clock had struck eleven in the morning. Only one missing woman had any connection to Eagle Ridge. Vivian Winchester had been a member since the age of sixteen. Her sister, Valerie—also a long-time member—had filed the missing persons report a week ago.

Eileen stared at the out-of-focus headshot of Vivian Winchester. The woman had it all: blonde hair, gray-blue eyes, beautiful bone structure, a slim build—*and* she could afford to buy *Joy* perfume by the barrel.

"What do we do now?" Zoe asked Eileen.

"Now I go talk to the sister."

Zoe grinned at Alfie. "She means *we*."

"I'll start the car," Eileen said.

Chapter Two

Winchester Manor was situated on Cypress Street in Shaughnessy Heights, one of the wealthiest neighborhoods in all of British Columbia. A twelve-foot, wrought iron fence and matching electric gate guarded the impressive Victorian mansion and its elegantly manicured lawn and gardens. Streaks of sunlight illuminated two stone gargoyles with sharp talons that gripped the tops of the gateposts. Gargoyle eyes, intimidating and unfriendly, peered down on all who dared to enter.

"I bet those look even creepier at night," Zoe said, leaning forward in the back seat of Eileen's rust-covered, pea-soup-green

Honda Civic. "They look like they're watching us."

Eileen repressed a shiver. "Not my kind of décor."

"Google says the house was built by billionaire software tycoon, Walter Winchester," Zoe said, reading from her new cell phone. "He designed the 6500-square-foot home for his second wife after they were married in 1979. Oh, this is sad. Mrs. Winchester died while visiting New York during 9-11. Her husband died in May 2014, and his children inherited the family home and fortune."

"Dem people are born with a silver spoon up der a—"

"Alfie!" Eileen frowned at the woman beside her. "Language."

From the back seat, Zoe let out a huff. "It's not like I haven't heard *ass* before, Eileen."

"Yeah, yeah, I know. But what kind of foster mom would I be if I don't chastise you"—Eileen glanced at Alfie—"or anyone else who swears around you?"

The older woman hung her head. "Sorry, Miss Eileen. I won't say *ass* no more."

Zoe snickered. "You just did."

Ignoring them, Eileen navigated a sharp

U-turn in the middle of the street and drove up to the gate, which housed a security panel with a numerical keypad. A red button marked "Speaker" caught her eye. She leaned out the window and pressed the button.

"Do you have an appointment?" a male voice asked in a bored tone.

"No," Eileen said. "I'm—"

"Please make an appointment by phone," Bored Guy said before hanging up.

She gritted her teeth and pressed the button again.

Bored Guy actually sighed. "Do you have an appointment?"

"I don't *need* an appointment. I'm a private investigator working with the police. I have some questions for Valerie Winchester regarding her sister, Vivian."

There was a long pause. Then the gate buzzed and opened inward.

"Wow," Zoe said. "I feel like we're going to meet the queen or something."

"Or something," Eileen muttered. She parked the car on the circular driveway. "You two stay here. Got it?"

Zoe pouted, while Alfie opened the canvas bag she never went anywhere without and proceeded to pull out the multicolored work of art she'd knitted.

"I'll see that Miss Zoe behaves," Alfie said.

"Maybe it's not Zoe I'm worried about."

Alfie shot her a wry look. "Don't you worry none 'bout me. I got some knittin' to do."

Eileen climbed out of the car and made her way to the formidable double doors. The fragrance of lilacs lingered close to the grand entrance, along with a scent that could only be described as "money." She peeked through the glass windows. The interior of the home appeared to be just as formidable as the exterior—Italian marble floor tiles, stone pillars, and a winding hardwood staircase that seemed to go on forever.

She pressed the doorbell, its pleasant melody resonating deep within the bones of the home. She peered through the glass in the door. An obscure form broke away from the shadows of the interior and moved closer. The door opened, revealing a white-haired man of indiscriminate age dressed in an expensive, tailored, gray suit and equally posh mauve silk tie.

"May I see your badge, please?" His British accent rolled fluidly off his tongue. This *wasn't* Bored Guy.

Eileen showed him her private investigator's card.

He waved her inside. "Miss Valerie awaits you in the drawing room. Please follow me."

Eileen resisted the urge to laugh at the pretentiousness of it all. *Drawing room? What the heck do people do in a drawing room, anyway?*

She entered the room, paused and sucked in a breath. Dark wood paneling covered the walls and built-in bookshelves, while crimson damask drapes hung down the sides of a large picture window that overlooked a floral garden setting.

"This was my father's favorite room," said the woman standing near the window, her back to Eileen. "I can still smell his cologne."

"I'm sorry for your loss."

The woman turned on one heel and gave her an anxious smile.

Early thirties, Eileen guessed.

Valerie Winchester commanded attention with her poise and beauty. Argillite-black hair had been cut into a stylish asymmetrical bob, and she had her sister's eyes and heart-shaped face. A simple gold chain with a diamond-studded infinity pendant draped her neck, diamonds twinkled on her earlobes, and on her right middle finger she wore a large gold signet ring inlaid with a black stone.

Valerie pointed to a chair. "Please, have a seat. I take it you're here about my sister's disappearance?"

"Not exactly, Miss Winchester." Eileen sat on the sofa, while Valerie took the armchair across from her. "I'm working on a case in conjunction with Vancouver Police, and your sister may or may not be involved."

Valerie frowned. "Have you found her?"

"Not yet. In your report you mention that you hadn't seen your sister for a few weeks. Is that odd?"

"We're very close, Vivian and I. But we do lead separate lives. She's a bit of a wild one, while I run our father's company."

"Do you know if anyone else saw your sister within the past three weeks?"

Valerie shook her head. "Sorry. No one seems to know where she's been or what she's been doing." Her voice shook. "I'm really worried. I've already lost my parents. I couldn't handle it if anything happened to Vivian." Tears welled in her eyes. "Please, find my baby sister and bring her home."

"I have the list of contacts you gave the police." Eileen handed her the paper. "Is there anyone else you can think of who may have had contact with Vivian in the past month?"

Valerie studied the list of names. "This is it."

"Has she ever done this before—taken off for long periods of time?"

"Sometimes. I may not hear from her for maybe a week, but we always catch up by phone, if nothing else." A tear trickled down the woman's face. "I'm scared something has happened to her."

"Does Vivian have any upcoming appointments you know about, or perhaps a place she visits routinely?"

"All her appointments are on her cell phone, which she has with her. Have the police found her phone?"

"Not yet. It can take some time."

"There's a nightclub she hangs out at on weekends. But everyone I've talked to there says she hasn't been by in weeks."

"What's the name?"

"After Midnight."

Eileen scribbled in a small notepad. She took a deep breath before continuing. "Do you have Vivian's hairbrush or toothbrush?"

Horror shot across Valerie's face. "Have you found a body?"

"No, but we need a DNA sample in case we find *any* trace of her," Eileen said, keeping her voice calm.

Valerie stood, one hand braced against the head of the chair. "I'll get her toothbrush."

After the woman left, Eileen wandered around the room. Though tastefully decorated in old man/old money décor, not a single photograph hung on the walls. She understood how grief after death could make a person want to hide those who have passed away. She'd done the same thing with Will's photos after her son's death. It had been too painful a reminder to see his smiling face every day. But grief eventually worked its way out, and she'd returned all the photos to their places just before Alfie and Zoe moved in.

Valerie returned with an electric toothbrush. "I hope this helps."

Eileen held out an open evidence bag. "Thank you."

"Vivian is my baby sister. She's a bit naïve at times, but everyone loves her. I can't see how anyone could hurt her."

"Is there anyone you can think of who

would benefit in any way if she were...out of the picture?"

"You mean as in financially?"

Eileen shrugged. "Sure."

"Well, our father left his fortune to both of us, equally. I suppose there could be someone out there who wants her half. But I don't know how they think they'll get it."

"Do you know if your sister has a will?"

"I'm not sure, but I can give you the name of our family lawyer. If Vivian left a will, then Patricia will know."

Valerie strode over to the desk and rummaged through the drawers. "Here's her card. Patricia Carmo. She's an excellent lawyer."

Eileen put the card in her jacket pocket. "Thank you. I'll contact her today. I understand you and your sister are members of Eagle Ridge Golf & Country Club. How do you like it there?"

"It's great. My family has been going there for years."

"Are you any good?"

"At golf? Not as good as Vivian is. But then I haven't had as much free time as she's had." Valerie chuckled. "I've never been too sure if she goes there to show everyone else up or for the eye candy."

"Eye candy?"

"There are a few very good-looking members at Eagle Ridge, not to mention some eligible bachelors."

"Neither you nor your sister are married?"

"Vivian was for a while. One of those flings that never should've started. Johnny Blake, former hockey hero. But he's been out of her life for about two years. As for me, I am far too busy running my father's empire to even think about serious dating." Her eyes held a trace of wistfulness. "Maybe one day."

"Do you have her ex-husband's contact info?"

Valerie flinched. "You think Johnny's responsible for—"

"Hold on. I'm looking into everyone and anyone who knows your sister. Including her exes."

"I lost track of Johnny after he and Vivian split up. My sister hasn't mentioned him in at least a year. He moved on. So did she. Is there anything else I can do to help?"

"I have one last request. Can I see Vivian's room?"

"Of course. Please follow me." Valerie led her back into the foyer and up the staircase. "My sister's suite is in the west wing."

Two steps inside Vivian's room, Eileen lurched to a halt and blinked. The decadence of the space overwhelmed her. Lush fabrics in silver and mauve tones decorated the windows and the king bed at the far end. Mahogany furniture that would look crowded in Eileen's bedroom appeared small in comparison to the spaciousness of the room. French doors opened to a private garden. An archway framed the entrance to Vivian's private library, while yet another doorway offered a view into the largest bathroom Eileen had ever seen.

"Wow, this is some bedroom suite."

"You should see her walk-in closet," Valerie said. "My sister has the most amazing shoe collection, including imports from around the globe."

Eileen gasped when Valerie opened a sliding door, revealing a closet to die for. "That's not a closet. That's another bedroom."

Valerie was right about the shoe collection. Shelves with small lights lined the back wall and both sides, with at least two-hundred pairs of fashionable designer shoes and boots.

Eileen picked up a silver stiletto and glanced at the brand. "Jimmy Choo. Way out of my price range."

"Every woman should own at least one pair of Jimmy Choo's shoes." Valerie attempted a smile. "That's what Vivian always says."

The bathroom's feature focus, an oversized glass-and-tile shower, stood in the center of the room. A two-person tub backed against a large window.

Eileen indicated the drawers in the vanity. "Do you mind?"

"No. Go ahead."

An assortment of cosmetics, creams and perfumes lined the shelves.

"Are you looking for something in particular?"

"I like to get a feel for who I'm looking for. Sometimes the answers are in the smallest details." Like the bottle of *Joy* that Eileen spotted amidst the fragrances. *And there's the connection!*

"One more thing," she said, retrieving her cell phone from her handbag. She flipped to the photo gallery. "Have you seen this scarf before?"

Valerie's face instantly drained of color. "That's my sister's."

"Are you sure?"

Valerie drifted toward a window. "I bought it for her when I was in Delhi last summer. Where did you find it?"

"Eagle Ridge Golf & Country Club."

The woman blew out a ragged breath. "Well, that makes sense. Vivian went to the club every week. Doesn't mean anything's happened to her though. She's just…missing."

"I think I'm done here."

Eileen followed Valerie downstairs and paused near the front door. "Thank you for your time, Ms. Winchester."

"Please find my sister. Vivian's all I've got."

"I'll get back to you if we get a lead or if I have more questions."

"Thank you, Detect—uh…I'm not sure what to call you."

"*Eileen* is fine." She handed Valerie a card. "Call me if you think of anything else that might be helpful."

Valerie swiped at a stray tear. "I will. Thank you, Eileen. And please…find Vivian before something awful happens to her."

Outside, Eileen made a beeline for the car. She almost reached it before she realized there were no occupants inside.

Damn it!

"Alfie and Zoe, where the heck are you?"

Shading her eyes from the late afternoon sun, she surveyed the grounds, praying Zoe hadn't talked Alfie into sneaking inside.

"Over here!" Zoe appeared from around the side of the house and waved at her. "We're talking to Edwin."

Eileen marched toward her. "You know you're not supposed to talk to strangers, Zoe. And I told you both to—"

"I know, I know. Don't blame Alfie. It was my idea to talk to him."

When Eileen reached Zoe, she saw Alfie talking to the older man who'd answered the door. *Edwin?* Watching them, she couldn't help but notice how Alfie's eyes had brightened. Whatever they were talking about, the woman seemed enamored.

"Eileen!" Alfie shouted. "Come meet Edwin."

"We already met."

Zoe nudged her. "You know, you can learn a lot about a family by talking to the help."

"You're too smart for your own good, kiddo."

Zoe rolled her eyes. "I'm helping. Isn't

that what you asked me to do?"

Eileen sighed. The kid had a point. "Fine, but next time I tell you to stay put, you stay put. Same goes for Alfie."

"I think she's got a crush on old Edwin there," Zoe said with a wide grin.

Alfie laughed at something the man said and completely ignored Eileen's gestures to get moving.

"Yup," Zoe snickered. "Alfie's in lo-ove."

"Car, now!" Eileen said between gritted teeth. "Alfie! We're leaving—with or without you."

She'd never seen the elderly black woman move so fast, and she hid a small smile when she saw Edwin watch Alfie's every move. Maybe Zoe was right. "Alfie, you have something to tell me?"

"Nope, Miss Eileen. I got nothin'." But the giddy expression on Alfie's face suggested   otherwise.

Chapter Three

Situated in the mountains of northeast Coquitlam, Eagle Ridge Golf & Country Club boasted an immaculate eighteen-hole course with challenging sand and water hazards. The course had a raw wilderness feel that appealed to nature lovers looking for a peaceful break from city life and stress. However, that afternoon, the bright yellow crime scene tape strung through the distant tree line screamed anything but fun and relaxation.

The club had multiple parking lots—one for members-only, one for guests and one for staff. Eileen hesitated for a moment before selecting the guest parking lot.

"What do we do first?" Zoe asked.

"We check in with the manager. Then we head to the crime scene."

"I don't got my walkin' shoes on, Miss Eileen."

"That's okay, Alfie. You can stay in the car, if you want."

"I've got my knittin' to keep me busy."

Eileen and Zoe climbed out and made their way to the clubhouse.

"Are you going to be all right with this?" Eileen asked the kid.

Zoe gave her the standard teenager eye roll. "I've seen worse. Remember?"

Eileen sighed. "Of course. So…what can you tell me about the manager?"

According to Zoe's internet search, Orest André had managed Eagle Ridge Golf & Country Club for more than two decades. In all that time, the only scandal he'd experienced occurred fifteen years earlier, when a young caddy and an older, married socialite were caught *in flagrante* in the greenskeeper's shed. The caddy was personally tossed out by the socialite's husband, a long-time member and wealthy philanthropist who'd donated over three million dollars to the club in the past ten years. As a result of the scandal, his marriage crumbled—along with his golf scores—and he passed away a few years later.

A small, bald man with hunched shoulders greeted Eileen with a tight smile and suspicious eyes framed by thick lenses that needed a good cleaning. His silver moustache shriveled when he noticed Zoe. With a weighty sigh, he ushered them into his sparsely-decorated office and closed the door.

"I appreciate you seeing me, Mr. André," Eileen said.

"Thank you for your discretion, Ms. Edwards." André ran a bony hand over his pale scalp. "Any news on what the heck is going on?"

"Nothing concrete yet, but we do know that one of your members has been reported missing. Vivian Winchester. The police are trying to locate her now."

"I heard about that."

"When was the last time you saw her?"

André thought for a moment. "At the Christmas party, I think. I don't mingle all that much with our members, but I do recall talking to one of the sisters briefly."

"I understand you have security cameras on the grounds."

André nodded. "Motion-sensor cameras. All eighteen holes are covered, plus the members-only, visitors and staff parking lots."

"What about the service roads?"

"There are two that pass through the backwoods behind the course, but neither is monitored by cameras. Our greenskeeper has been here longer than I have—and no one else is supposed to use those roads." André caught sight of Zoe's scornful arched brow. "In hindsight, I realize that doesn't mean someone *won't*."

"Any indication the camera equipment has been tampered with?" Eileen asked.

"Not to my knowledge. Then again, technology passed me by over twenty years ago, which is why I had a few copies of the tape made by an associate—for investigators like you." He handed her a flash drive. "This one covers the past four weeks, all cameras. There's also a copy of our guest registration for the past month."

"Are there cameras *inside* the clubhouse?"

The man nodded. "In the hallways only. We respect our members' privacy too much to monitor their every move, although we did put one of those scanner thingies above the shop door."

When Eileen frowned, Zoe said, "He means the door alarm that goes off if you try to leave with something you stole."

The not-so-innocent expression on the teen's face told Eileen the kid was far too familiar with "scanner thingies" *and* shoplifting.

"Thank you for your time, Mr. André." Eileen stood and steered Zoe toward the door.

"I hope you find the Winchester girl," Orest André replied. "Alive and well."

"So do I." A tentacle of fear tugged at Eileen's heart. *Alive and well.*

Outside, smoky clouds churned above, building in volume over the mountains. The occasional fat raindrop hit Eileen as they traipsed past the clubhouse and made their way to the golf cart rentals.

"It's a good thing Alfie decided not to come with us," she said to Zoe. "Hopefully the weather will cooperate."

She flashed her ID at the blue-eyed, twenty-something attendant whose nametag read: *MAT.* Beside her, Zoe snickered.

"What's so funny?"

"His name. It's like…door mat."

The young man grinned. "Some

dumbass in the office can't spell."

Zoe reached into her pocket then held up a pen. "Lean down. I'll fix it for you." She added the missing T to the end of MAT.

"Thanks, kid," Matt said with a wink.

Zoe blushed and pocketed the pen. "No big deal."

"I have a few questions." Air hissed between Eileen's teeth. "If you don't mind."

"No problem. Been a slow day today, what with the cops here again."

"You work here long?"

"Just over a year."

"Do you know Vivian Winchester?"

"Everyone knows Vivian."

"When's the last time you saw her?"

He scratched the overgrown stubble on his chin. "Uh…maybe three weeks ago. She was at the driving range, practicing her backspin. That girl's got a great swing."

"You see anyone hanging around her?"

Matt shrugged. "She usually has a few cling-ons." He grinned. "Even in sportswear, Vivian Winchester is one hot babe."

Eileen frowned. *Vivian may also be one hot corpse.* "What about her instructor?"

"Chip?"

Eileen raised a brow. "And his last name?"

"Mulligan."

"Are you kidding me? Chip Mulligan?"

Matt shrugged. "Like Chip says, he was born for golf. His old man, Dirk Mulligan, competed in the Masters a few years back."

"Is Chip here now?"

"He'll be on shift in about an hour, I think." Matt patted the side of a pristine silver cart. "Until then, you need a ride out to the crime scene, right? This little baby is usually reserved for pro players."

"Well, *that* I am not."

Matt grinned. "Mini-golf, huh?"

"That's about my speed." Eileen climbed into the golf cart. "I'll bring this back when we're done."

"Don't get a speeding ticket," Matt joked.

With Zoe seated beside her, Eileen maneuvered the cart past the driving range and onto the green. The drive to the back nine took some time, and some dodging of rough patches, but they finally made it. Woodlands loomed in the background, shadowy tentacles flickering between bushes and heavy, fringed cedars.

"Can I drive back when we're done?" Zoe asked.

"Sorry, kiddo. We're here on business,

remember?"

"Yeah, yeah." Zoe sulked a moment then said, "At least I get to help you look for clues."

"Here's how this is going to play out, Zoe. Once we're behind the tape, you're going to stay behind me at all times. Don't go wandering off. And don't touch anything."

Zoe pouted. "But what if I see something suspicious?"

"You tell me, and I'll check it out. Deal?"

"Fine." Zoe drew out that one word as though it had two syllables.

Minutes later, Eileen noticed a uniformed rookie leaning against a tree in the distance. She didn't recognize him from her time at VPD. She parked the cart and approached by foot. "Constable Martin sent me. I'm the PI."

The young officer nodded. "He told me you'd be putting in an appearance. Eileen Edwards, right? You're a legend around the station." He grinned, flashing perfect, white teeth. "Chris Antoniuk. I moved here from Edmonton with my wife about six months ago."

"Ah! Traded in your parka for a

raincoat?"

Antoniuk laughed. "And my snow blower for an umbrella. Who's the kid?"

"I'm not a kid," Zoe grumbled. "I'm a teenager."

Eileen sighed. "She's with me."

Antoniuk frowned. "It's against protocol to have kids visit an active crime scene."

"I know. Call this a family field trip. Now where to?"

"Just follow the tape, ma'am."

Eileen grimaced. If there was one thing she couldn't stand, it was being called "ma'am."

Heeding the rookie's advice, she made her way through the trees, with Zoe following close on her heels. Fresh cut branches suggested someone had recently cleared the path. Boot prints—police issue, by the treads—and yellow tape marked the way along the damp, twisty trail.

A bird shrieked directly above them, and Eileen faltered, almost twisting her ankle. She had to admire the bald eagle circling leisurely overhead. With wings spread wide, it drifted majestically along the currents. A few yards away, a murder of crows perched along a dead tree branch. Their beady eyes followed Eileen.

"Over there!" Zoe shouted.

Five yellow evidence markers sat on the ground below a fiery maple tree.

Eileen turned to Zoe. "Stay here. I'm going to check it out."

The eagle screeched, as if in answer. A low rumble of thunder followed, and Eileen cursed beneath her breath. A rainstorm would wash away any remaining evidence. *I'd better hurry.*

Moving closer to the maple tree, she scanned the area for anything out of the ordinary. She came up empty. No flickers of metal, no pieces of fabric—nothing. She eyed the ground, which had been trampled by crime scene investigators and the boy who'd found the evidence. She crouched down, lifting a marker a few inches off the ground. The tented plastic protected a substantial pool of coagulated blood and a few faint smears where the evidence team had most likely taken samples.

"This is definitely the place," Zoe said over Eileen's shoulder.

"Jesus, don't creep up on me like that. You almost knocked me over."

"Sorry." Zoe gave her a sheepish grin. "That's blood, isn't it?"

"Yup."

"Blood from the person who lost that tooth?"

"That's my guess," Eileen said, setting the marker down.

"That much blood makes this the primary crime scene, right?"

Eileen straightened. "You've been watching too many violent TV shows."

"But I'm right, aren't I?"

Eileen sighed. "The victim was attacked here, but other than the blood, there's nothing else, not even a trail."

"What about that feather?" Zoe asked. "Is that a clue?"

Eileen followed her gaze. A long brown feather rested between two branches of a nearby bush. She picked up the feather and noticed coagulated blood near the tip. "There's blood on it, but that's it." She bagged it anyway. "Not much of a clue."

Zoe beamed a smile. "Except you forgot something."

"What?"

"To look up."

"All I see is that blasted eagle. Its squawking is giving me a headache."

"She has a nest around here somewhere. That's why she's circling so low and making so much noise."

"How do you know that?"

"Something Old Pete taught me."

Back when Alfie had been her confidential informant on the streets, Eileen had met Pete Hutchins, a military soldier suffering from PTSD—a familiar face on the streets of Vancouver until he passed away. He'd also become a surrogate father to Zoe and a trusted friend to Alfie.

Eileen shaded her eyes. The eagle dipped low into the trees then soared higher. A second eagle appeared. "What would Old Pete say now?"

Zoe's smile widened. "That those two are mates. Then he'd say, 'Eagles are very protective of their young.'"

"What the heck does that mean?"

"Means we have to search for the nest. There might be something in it."

"But what about the eagles. They might attack if they're protecting their young."

"The eaglets should be out of the nest by now."

Eileen gave her a gentle nudge. "How did you get so smart?"

"I watch too many violent TV shows."

"Smart ass."

"Um, you just swore."

Eileen sighed. "Okay, smarty-pants.

Let's find that nest."

"I think I already did." Zoe strode over to a Douglas fir. "It's way up there. See?"

The kid was right. A massive eagle's nest rested between branches near the top of the fir.

Eileen estimated the nest to be perched between branches at least thirty feet from the ground. "We'll need a ladder with an extension."

"Nope," Zoe said, touching the rough bark of the trunk. "This'll be a piece of cake."

One second Zoe stood beside Eileen; the next she scrambled up the tree. The kid's nimbleness impressed her. The branchless bottom half of the trunk made for a smooth climb, but Eileen still held her breath.

"See?" Zoe called out. "I'm almost there."

"I don't think this is a good idea. You might fall. Come back down."

Zoe clung to the tree. "Jeez, Eileen, I could do this in my sleep. Didn't you ever climb trees when you were young? Or don't you remember that far back?"

"Funny." Eileen released a soft groan. "If you fall, I'll be the worst foster mother in history."

"I won't fall. I climb trees at Stanley Park all the time."

Eileen shifted closer to the tree, positioning herself directly under Zoe. If the girl fell…well, she'd do her best to catch her—or be squashed in the process. Not even the thin blanket of seed cones and needles beneath the tree would help cushion a fall. She blew out a breath once she saw Zoe reach the nest.

"Crap," Eileen muttered. "I should've given you some gloves and a couple of evidence bags."

"Already got bags." Zoe pulled a plastic bag from her jacket.

"Where did you get those?"

"From the glove compartment of your car. You always keep extras in there."

Yeah, this kid is far too smart for her own good.

"If you find anything in the nest, try to pick it up with a twig or the bag. And be careful!"

"I will." A second later, Zoe hollered, "I think I found more blood."

Eileen paced beneath the fir tree. If the victim's blood *was* in that nest then the eagle must have disturbed the bloody mess below. Maybe the bird had picked up the tooth or scarf and then dropped it. But why? It wasn't as though a human molar or a silk scarf were all that heavy.

Eileen froze. *Perhaps the eagle had been interrupted.*

Minutes later, Zoe landed on solid ground. She handed two small bags to Eileen and gave her a wide smile. "I found a button too."

Eileen examined the button in the bag. Black, plastic, flat, no markings except for a speck or two of what looked like dried blood. "Could be from anyone."

"I found it *in* the blood. Maybe it came from that woman."

The other bag held several small twigs, each about four inches long and splattered with droplets of crimson.

"I believe you're right, kiddo. This is most definitely blood."

Zoe gave her a somber look. "How much you wanna bet it's that missing woman's?"

Eileen shook her head. "Come on. We've got more people to interview."

Chapter Four

"Great ride," Eileen said, parking the golf cart in the space Matt indicated.

"You're in luck," he said. "Chip got here about twenty minutes ago, which is really bizarre because that dude never shows up early."

"Can you tell me where he is?"

"Sure thing. I believe he's on the fourth hole." Matt handed her a map of the course and pointed. "Around here."

Zoe and Eileen returned to the cart and set out across the grass.

"I don't get this whole golf-is-a-sport thing," Zoe said. "It's slow, no real action. They spend more time walking than hitting the ball. Looks pretty lame."

"I hear ya," Eileen murmured. "Maybe they know something we don't."

They passed various golfers along the way, not one under seventy years old.

"This here place is where old folks come to die," Zoe drawled.

Eileen frowned. *Maybe not just old folks.*

"I think that's him." Zoe pointed to a towering figure a few yards away.

Chip Mulligan was Hollywood gorgeous—like the blonde with him. She looked about thirty-five and had a hefty pair of surgical enhancements that were getting in the way of her swing. Wearing an Eagle Ridge cap, the rim turned to the back, Mulligan looked far too comfortable with his arms around the woman as he whispered in her ear.

As the cart approached, Eileen took in the instructor's striking features. Mulligan was the epitome of "tall, dark and handsome." She pegged him at about thirty, well over six feet tall, with bulging biceps that rippled when he swung. He beamed perfect white teeth in her direction, and Eileen had a strange and sudden desire to take golf lessons.

Clearing her throat, she pulled the cart to a stop and disembarked, while Zoe hung back. "Mr. Mulligan? I'm a private investigator working in conjunction with the police." She held up her ID. "Can we talk...privately?" She flicked a dismissive look in the blonde's direction.

"Meet you at the next hole," Mulligan told his student. "Take the cart."

"Don't be long," the woman said breathily. "I don't want to lose my...momentum." She climbed into a club cart and drove off.

"So..." Mulligan said, flashing another blinding smile, "what can I do for you?"

"I understand you've been instructing Vivian Winchester. When did you see her last?"

Mulligan scratched his chin. "Maybe two weeks ago."

"You didn't think this strange?"

Mulligan shrugged. "I figured she took off jet-setting somewhere hot and tropical and didn't have time to let me know. Vivian's always on the go. It's not the first time she's disappeared."

"When was that?"

"She went AWOL for part of 2016. No one knew why, not even that sister of hers."

Disdain coated his words.

"You have an issue with Valerie Winchester?"

"Haven't seen *her* in months, but yeah. Good ole Val the Virgin is Vivian's jailer. A goddamn frickin' buzzkill." His gaze drifted toward Zoe, who sat in the cart, eyes glued to her cell phone. "Sorry. I'll try to keep the language clean."

"I appreciate that," Eileen said dryly.

"Vivian isn't like her sister. She's more...vivacious, exciting, fearless."

"Sounds like you and Vivian are more than friends."

Mulligan held up his hands in surrender. "You got me. *And* about two dozen other guys within a fifty-mile radius of Vancouver." He snickered. "Probably a few women too."

"Are you in love with Vivian?"

"Nah," he scoffed. "We're just friends with benefits. I'm not looking for anything long term. Neither is she."

"Do you know if she has any enemies?"

"I'm sure Vivian has pissed off more than a few people. Take that lawyer of hers, for one, Patricia Carmo."

"What about her?"

"Vivian swears the woman is skimming

off the Winchester fortune."

"Did she have any proof?"

Chip Mulligan hesitated.

"Listen," she said. "Vivian Winchester is missing. Her sister is terrified that something has happened to her. If you have any information that could help VPD find Vivian, then you need to tell me."

"Well…I don't know that this'll help you, but Vivian told me the lawyer couldn't account for nearly twenty-five thousand dollars. It somehow disappeared. I suggested going to another lawyer, but that bitch has been with their family since forever. And Vivian said she'd look into it herself, so I let it go."

Eileen circled "$25,000" in her notebook. "Did Vivian confront her lawyer about her suspicions?"

Mulligan nodded. "Yeah. Shit lotta good that did."

A glance over one shoulder told Eileen that Zoe was occupied with reading something on her cell phone. "Why's that?"

"Lawyer denied it, of course. Vivian threatened to fire her, but Valerie stepped in and smoothed everything over." He paused for a long moment then added, "Maybe *she* stole the money."

"Why would Valerie do that? She's supposed to be the responsible one."

"Haven't got a clue. All I know is that Vivian was fed up because her sister controlled the money. And the lawyer lady? Vivian once told me she suspected her father had had an affair with her."

"With Patricia Carmo, you mean."

"Don't know if it's true, but yeah."

"Hey, Eileen?" Zoe hollered. "Can we go yet?"

"In a minute." To Mulligan she said, "Is there anything else you can tell me about Vivian. Like where she'd go, if she wanted to disappear?"

"Vivian Winchester has friends all across Canada and the US. She could virtually hide anywhere. Especially if she took that money."

With Mulligan's words ringing in her head, she thanked him and climbed back into the cart. Starting the engine, she gave a nod and watched as he crossed the green.

"He's kinda hot," Zoe said. "For an older dude."

"Zoe!"

However, the kid had a point. Chip Mulligan was highly charismatic, beyond attractive and a definite playboy—exactly the kind of man a woman like Vivian Winchester would pursue, from what everyone said.

"We're leaving, kiddo."

Zoe's exaggerated groan of relief followed them.

"I thought you wanted to help me with this case?"

"I do, but that was bo-o-ring."

As they reached the staff parking lot, Eileen wrapped an arm around Zoe and hugged her. Sometimes she forgot that Zoe was a hormonal teenage girl, complete with mood swings and PMS. Zoe was also a child of the streets, where action happened every five minutes.

"You can always stay at home if you're bored."

"But I wanna help."

Eileen sighed. "Then we'll have to figure out the best way you can do so."

"I've got skills," Zoe said in a mysterious tone. "Things I learned on the street."

"Let's keep that between us," Eileen warned. "And if I need your kind of…uh…skillset, I'll ask you. Right now, I simply want your observations."

"Well, I can tell you one thing…"

"What's that?"

"That instructor dude is giving more than golf lessons. Did you see the way he was *teaching*"—Zoe made air quotes with her fingers—"that lady?"

Zoe was right. Mulligan had wrapped his arms around the blonde, his forearms grazing her fake Double-Ds and his lower extremity pressed tightly against the woman's buttocks. It was a wonder the poor woman could breathe.

Maybe VPD has a file on the guy.

Chip Mulligan made it to the top of her potential suspects list. Patricia Carmo, next.

With the clubhouse in her rear-view mirror, Eileen veered off Eagle Ridge Drive and turned down a gravel road, one of the unmonitored service roads Orest André had mentioned. As the car lurched and moaned, she navigated the potholes as best she could and studied the area. Thick underbrush and tall, leafy trees made for a million hiding places.

"We lost, Miss Eileen?" Alfie piped up, breaking Eileen's concentration.

"No, we should be behind the golf course." The road came to an abrupt end, and she slammed on the brakes. "Jesus! A little warning would've helped."

Eileen parked the car and climbed out. With hands on hips, she studied the area, noting deep tire ruts in the gravel. Someone had recently transported a heavy load. Crouching, she inspected the ruts. Rain had destroyed any definition of the tread marks.

She called Rick Martin on her cell phone. "I assume VPD checked out the two service roads behind Eagle Ridge. You find anything?"

"Nada."

"Take any casts of the tire treads?"

"One, but it was too degraded by rain to get much. All we know is that a heavy truck with wide tires used the road in the past week, and that fits the description of the club's service truck."

"Well, I doubt someone carried Vivian Winchester away without some kind of vehicle."

"I agree, but we had CSU go over the truck. If someone used it, other than the greenskeeper, there's no trace. All club vehicles are washed and vacuumed routinely in one of the outbuildings."

"Ah, shit."

"My sentiments exactly."

With a sigh, Eileen said, "I'm on my

way to the station."

Chapter Five

The downtown police station still had that familiar stench, a pungent potpourri of strong coffee, day-old donuts, stale alcohol and sour vomit. All the odor-eliminating sprays in the world couldn't make the air more palatable.

Alfie had opted to take the bus back home, so she wouldn't miss *Days of Our Lives*. Eyes gleaming with excitement, Zoe begged to stay with Eileen.

She left Zoe in Larry's empty office, rather than the waiting area currently crowded with the hookers, drunks and other miscreants. "Don't go anywhere. I'll be back in ten minutes."

According to the female desk sergeant on duty, Constable Vigo Ducci—"Dutch" to his friends and "VD" to his enemies—was in the break room down the hall, imbibing in his favorite activities: drinking coffee and licking the icing off the donuts. If Eileen didn't at least say hello to the man, she'd never hear the end of it.

When she entered the break room, a towering hulk swept her up in his arms and twirled her around like a child. "Put me down, Dutch. You don't want me to puke all over your uniform, do you?"

A low, rumbling laugh answered.

"I guess you're feeling better," she said as he set her down.

"Thank God. No more desk duty for me."

"Unless you shoot yourself in the ass again."

Dutch did an exaggerated eye roll. "How many times do I have to tell people? It was an *accident*."

"You stick to your story."

They were interrupted by an attractive, muscular officer with a frown on his clean-shaven face. Dutch bowed out silently and returned to his desk.

Months out of a two-year undercover

stint with the Demonios de Los Muertos gang, Constable Rick Martin greeted her with a curt nod. "Have any luck at Eagle Ridge?"

"Actually, yes."

She gave him the flash drive. "Security camera footage from Eagle Ridge."

Rick scowled. "You steal this?"

"I do have ways of getting evidence without resorting to theft. The manager offered it; I accepted. He also gave me a copy of the guest list."

"Luis and I will review the footage. Want me to send you a copy by email?"

"Sure."

Next, she handed Martin the evidence bags from the eagle's nest. He studied the blood-spattered button. "Do I want to know how you got this out of an eagle's nest?"

Eileen chuckled. "One word. *Zoe.*"

"The kid? You could've waited for us to send someone."

"Unless you were sending the *Chicago Fire* team, I wasn't willing to wait. Besides, it started raining, and Zoe climbed up that tree before I could stop her."

"Maybe I'll leave that out of the report."

"Zoe collected the evidence with my instruction. Nothing is tainted. And before I forget, the sister gave me this." Eileen dropped the bag containing Vivian Winchester's toothbrush on the table.

"I'll get this to the lab and put a rush on DNA."

"What next?"

Martin studied her for a moment. "I can take it from here."

Eileen shrugged. "I'm curious why I was asked to assist. Seems like you could've handled the missing persons files on your own."

The man turned away. "Norman thinks I'm too hard-assed to handle questioning a woman." Bitterness crept into every word. "Undercover work doesn't allow for much sensitivity, so he's probably right."

She struggled for a reply. "Larry always watches out for his crew. That's all."

"I don't need someone watching my every move to see if I mess up."

"Mart—*Rick*, no one's waiting for you to mess up. Except maybe you. But if you need help, I'm here."

Eileen walked out of the break room, cursing beneath her breath. She'd never worked with Martin when she'd been on the force, but she'd heard of him. No one else had been able to get close to the gang leader of the DLM. Martin's bravery had been well documented, but only a handful of people knew how much undercover work had cost him. His wife had taken off with his children—moved to Winnipeg, of all places. The divorce cost him everything.

She felt bad for the man. He was only doing his job.

Eileen flexed her right hand and immediately regretted it. Pain sliced though her thumb and index finger, radiating down to her wrist. A barely visible scar below the knuckle of her right index finger reminded her that the job had cost her, too.

When she entered Larry's office, she found Zoe slumped in a chair, her feet up on the cluttered desk. "Zoe! Feet down!"

"Don't worry, I didn't mess up his reports or anything. But you really need to tell Detective Norman to change his password. It's way too easy to guess."

Eileen crooked her finger. The girl rolled her eyes and stood. With a guilty glance toward the doorway, Zoe brushed off faint traces of dirt her running shoes had left behind on Larry's desk. "Oops, sorry."

They left Larry's office and stepped inside the elevator. Eileen pressed the button for the underground parkade, pondering her next move. The doors began to close, but a hand reached out, and Rick Martin stepped inside.

"I was thinking..." he began sheepishly. "I *could* use your help—if you'll accept my apology for my rudeness."

She smiled. "No apology needed. What would you like me to do?"

Instead of heading home, Eileen drove back to Shaughnessy Heights.

"What's the plan?" Zoe asked from the passenger seat.

"This is a highly sensitive matter. With the evidence we've already collected, we know *something* has happened to Vivian Winchester. I need to prepare her sister."

"Must be hard to lose a sister."

Not as hard as it is to lose a son.

Eileen recalled Will's smile. A drunk driver had deprived her of seeing her sixteen-year-old's smile daily...or hearing his laugh. She heard it in her dreams, though. Will would live forever in her mind and heart.

"You look sad," Zoe said, patting her arm. "You're thinking about Will, aren't you?"

Eileen cleared her throat. "The world is

so much smaller without him. I miss
everything about him. But I'm blessed to
have you and Alfie in my life. And for that,
I'm very grateful."

She maneuvered the vehicle into the
turning lane. They were a block from
Winchester Manor when she spotted a sleek
black sedan leaving the gates. Valerie was
on the move, and she seemed to be in a
hurry.

Curious, Eileen turned the car around
and followed.

"Is that her up ahead?" Zoe asked.

"Yeah. I want to see where she's going."

Twenty minutes later, the black sedan
pulled into a parking spot outside a strip of
luxury gift and service shops. Eileen
managed to finagle her car into a spot five
cars down. She watched Valerie climb out of
the sedan and enter a clothing store. Ten
minutes later, the woman exited with a
bright aqua shopping bag. Valerie headed
back to her car, then paused as though she'd
forgotten something, turned and went inside
the salon next door.

Sure the woman would be a while,
Eileen dialed Martin's number. "Any luck in
getting the warrant for Patricia Carmo and
the Winchesters' financials?"

"I'm waiting on Judge Rafferty," Martin said.

"Looks like you drew the short straw." Eileen knew Arnold Rafferty from several of her past cases. Rafferty had a reputation as a hard-ass, and he moved slower than a sloth. "I'll keep my fingers crossed."

"Better cross everything." Martin made a sound that may have been a laugh.

"She's leaving!" Zoe interrupted from the passenger seat.

"I have to go," Eileen said to Martin. "I'll call you later with a status report."

"You heading to the Manor?"

"I was, but we took a little detour. Nothing exciting. We'll chat later, Rick."

Hanging up, she watched Valerie Winchester return to her vehicle, two colorful shopping bags in hand.

"I guess when your sister's missing, you go shopping," Eileen muttered, more to herself than Zoe.

She shifted the car into reverse and backed up a foot. *Crap, this spot is tight!*

She hauled on the worn steering wheel and drove forward slowly, giving the van in front of her a light love-tap. She cursed under her breath. A few seconds of back-and-forth action finally produced results, and Eileen inched the car out of the tight spot and into the lane.

"You should buy a new car," Zoe said. "One that parks itself."

"People really need to stop harping about my car. It works."

"Some days. Or maybe it's just the *driver*."

"One day you'll be in the driver's seat, and we'll see how good *you* are."

"Old Pete said I was a great driver."

Eileen tamped back a curt reply. "We'll look at getting you in for lessons next year." She shivered at the thought of Zoe behind the steering wheel. *Do all parents feel this way?*

"She's turning right at the next light," Zoe said, tapping the window.

A white-panel bread truck blocked Eileen's view, but she turned right when she reached the intersection. Three vehicles ahead, the sedan turned left into an alley. That, alone, seemed suspicious.

What the heck is Valerie doing?

When Eileen turned into the alley, the sedan was gone.

"Maybe she saw us," Zoe said.

Eileen frowned. "Maybe." She inched the car down the alley. *Damn! Where did she go?*

They drove around the block three times.

With a sigh, Eileen said, "Since she's not at home yet, the next stop is the lawyer's."

Chapter Six

The business card Valerie had given her listed an address in downtown Vancouver. The Montgomery, Carmo and Singh building was insignificant in comparison to the oxygen-deprived skyscrapers two blocks away.

As Eileen pulled into the underground parkade beneath the law offices, she wondered whether Patricia Carmo had heard from Vivian recently.

"Can I come with you?" Zoe unfastened her seatbelt.

"Yes. You can sit in the waiting room, but no distractions."

They climbed out of the car, and Eileen

took stock of their surroundings. She abhorred underground parkades. Dim lighting and shadowed angles provided too many hiding places.

Gripping Zoe's arm, she directed the girl toward the elevator. When Eileen stepped inside, Zoe's hand hovered eagerly over the panel of buttons. "Which floor?"

"Seventh."

The girl smiled. Kids could find pleasure in the simplest things, even pushing an elevator button.

Arriving at the designated floor, they followed the sign to two floor-to-ceiling glass doors. Adjacent to the doors stood a chrome and glass table that featured a crystal vase filled with long-stemmed birds of paradise, one of Eileen's favorite flowers.

As they approached, the door on the right opened.

"Cool," Zoe whispered.

"Remember what I said."

Eileen made her way to the main lobby. A mid-twenties, redheaded woman sitting at the reception desk said something into the headset and plucked a clump of white fuzz from the sleeve of her tailored jacket. When she hung up, Eileen approached.

The receptionist peered up at her from

behind small aqua-colored fashion frames. "May I help you?"

"I don't have an appointment, but I'm here to see Patricia Carmo—on a police matter."

The receptionist's eyes widened. "Lucky for you, Ms. Carmo isn't in a meeting." She pushed a button and spoke into a headset. "There's a police officer here to see you."

Eileen almost corrected her, but closed her mouth. It wasn't *her* mistake, after all.

"Ms. Carmo will see you now," the receptionist said, standing. "Right this way."

Eileen followed her down the hallway, envying the young woman's toned arms and legs. Maybe a gym membership was included with the reception job. Eileen had tried a few gyms in the past, but they seemed to attract buff men with bulging biceps or skinny women running marathons on the treadmill. She could barely manage a brisk walk on the contraption. She'd let her last gym membership expire after visiting twice and feeling out of her element. Besides, she didn't have trendy exercise wear, like the younger gals. No, she'd stick to trudging the backyard and parks in her tattered track pants.

Glass walls and windows and natural

sunlight seemed to follow her everywhere. Seven stories up gave her a decent view of the city, though part of the view was obstructed by taller buildings. In the sunlight, Vancouver gleamed like a star dropped from the heavens. A financial and business hub of the world, the overcrowded city had nowhere else to go but up.

At the far end of the floor, Patricia Carmo's office boasted a magnificent view of the outside world. The minimalistic décor of the office gave no substantial clues about its inhabitant or her personality. No plants, no personal photos, just a lonely Keurig machine on the counter along the inner wall. At the opposite end, an electric ceramic warmer melted scented wax that fragranced the air with vanilla, coconut and a hint of sandalwood.

"Thank you for agreeing to see me on such short notice," Eileen said to the silver-haired woman seated behind a sleek, modern desk.

Patricia Carmo stood. "Nice to meet you, Detective Edwards." She gave a dismissive nod to the receptionist.

"Actually, I'm not a cop," Eileen said. "I'm a private investigator."

"Please, have a seat. How can I help

you?"

"I'm looking into a possible connection between a case I'm working on and the disappearance of one of your clients, Vivian Winchester."

"Oh, dear. Vivian…yes, that's a sad one. Her sister, Valerie, contacted me about a week ago because she hadn't heard from Vivian in some time. Have you found her? Is she okay?"

"We have nothing concrete yet. However, I'm new to Vivian's case and wondered if you might have additional information."

"I don't know how I can help you. I haven't spoken with Vivian in months."

"I understand their father left his fortune to the two sisters. Was there anyone else who might think they should've benefited instead?"

"You mean like illegitimate children or women on the side?" Carmo gave her a wry smile. "No, their father was infatuated with their mother. Walt never would've stepped out of line. At least not to my knowledge, and I've been the Winchester family lawyer for over three decades."

"Mr. Winchester left a will?"

"Yes. I can get you a copy of it, if you'd

like."

"You realize I don't have a court order."

Carmo shrugged. "If it helps find Vivian, then I'm positive she'd want me to show you." She pushed a button on her phone. "Liz, bring me Vivian Winchester's file." To Eileen, she said, "Would you like some coffee while we wait?"

"No, thank you. I'm good."

The receptionist made an appearance a few minutes later, a hefty brown folder in hand. She placed it on the desk then left.

"Here it is," Carmo said, combing through the documents in the folder. She slid a stack of pages toward Eileen. "As you can see, he kept things fairly simple. In the event of his death, all debts would be paid off and the family fortune split equally between his two daughters."

"And what if Vivian passes away?"

"Then the entire fortune goes to Valerie."

Eileen raised a brow. "She'd inherit everything?"

"She would." Carmo folded her hands on the desk. "I know what you're thinking, Ms. Edwards, but I can assure you, Valerie would never hurt Vivian. Valerie is set with more money than she ever could spend in a lifetime. She doesn't need her sister's share."

"Perhaps Valerie has debts you don't know about."

Carmo chuckled. "Not Valerie Winchester. She's the responsible one, the workaholic. And she's been like a mother to Vivian. Besides, I handle her investment portfolio. Trust me, she's set for life. If either sister were in trouble financially, I'd be the first to know."

"What about Vivian? How responsible is she?"

"Vivian loves to shop. There were a few incidences of overspending, but nothing severe. If she needed more funds for something important, Valerie would eventually approve the payment. Family comes first with the Winchesters. Always has, always will."

"Do you recall if Valerie mentioned anything to you about Eagle Ridge Golf & Country Club?"

"The Winchesters have spent a small fortune at Eagle Ridge. The girls practically grew up on the fairway. They even competed at the Canadian Women's Amateur Championship. Neither won, but they finished well."

Eileen scribbled in the notebook she always kept in her jacket pocket. "To your knowledge, is there anyone who has ever threatened either sister?"

Patricia Carmo tucked her hair behind one ear. "No one I can think of."

"I understand Vivian was briefly married. Any animosity between her and her ex?"

"Their divorce was amicable. I handled the paperwork. Johnny didn't want anything from Vivian. He had his own money, though not as substantial as Vivian's. I think they were both relieved to see the marriage dissolved. Afterward, Johnny up and moved back east somewhere. New York, maybe. Far as I know, he's still there." Carmo pressed the intercom button. "Liz, make Ms. Edwards a copy of Walter Winchester's will."

The receptionist swept into the room, plucked the folder off the desk and exited the office without a word. When she reappeared five minutes later, she handed a warm stack of papers to Eileen.

Carmo stood. "I assume we're done?"

Eileen nodded. "Thank you, Ms. Carmo. I appreciate your time."

"Anything to help the Winchester girls.

Liz, please see Ms. Edwards out."

Eileen paused in the doorway. "Oh, I almost forgot…"

"Yes?"

"An associate of Vivian's suggested that a large sum of money went missing from—"

"Let me interrupt you right there," Carmo said, holding up a hand. "I did *not* take money from my clients. And it was *not* my mistake. Besides, Valerie has already taken care of everything."

"The money was recovered?"

Carmo shook her head. "No, but I don't have it."

"Can you tell me what happened?"

"Someone withdrew twenty-five thousand dollars via a check made out to cash. My signature's on it, but I promise you, I never signed it. My office was broken into last year. The police were called, but nothing seemed out of place."

"When did you notice the missing money?"

"A week after police closed that investigation due to lack of evidence. I was going to report the theft, but Valerie didn't want the scandal—and to be honest, neither did I. She decided to let it go. I think she believes Vivian took the money."

"Pretty forgiving."

"Valerie has a heart of gold. Vivian is unreliable and immature for her age. She believes the entire word revolves around her." Carmo's lips thinned. "Fact is, Vivian has always lived in Valerie's shadow. But those sisters love each other."

"Love can make people do strange things," Eileen murmured.

"Both girls have been given a company Visa with a hefty limit. As I mentioned before, they don't need to steal their own money. You'll realize this once the police get their warrant for the Winchester financials tomorrow." When she saw Eileen's surprised confusion, she added, "I know how this works."

"Then why didn't you just give them the documents?"

"I'm a lawyer," Carmo said with a grin. "I have to follow legal protocol when it comes to my clients' money. Besides, when do we ever make things easy for anyone other than our clients?"

The lawyer had a point.

Eileen thanked her for her time and headed back to the lobby.

"Shall I book a follow-up appointment for you?" the receptionist asked.

"No, but I might be back tomorrow."

Zoe stood when Eileen approached. "We're done here, kiddo."

"Where to next?"

"Home." Eileen raised a hand when Zoe began to scowl. "Don't argue. It's getting late, and I'm hungry. We'll get takeout on the way. You can pick."

Zoe's scowl morphed into a grin. "KFC?"

Eileen gave a nod. "We've got a date with the Colonel."

After fighting rush-hour traffic and enduring the distorted speech of a kid who could barely speak English at the drive-through, Eileen set the bag with the bucket of chicken on the kitchen counter. A quick peek in the other bag revealed that the KFC kid had accidentally given them two potato salads. At least he hadn't forgotten the gravy. Otherwise, there'd be hell to pay.

"After supper I have to make some phone calls in my office. But first, I wanted to thank you both for your help today."

"Don't you go thankin' me," Alfie reprimanded. "You gave me a home an' regular meals. Least I can do is help out now an' den."

Zoe tugged on Eileen's shirtsleeve. "Can we help again tomorrow?"

"We'll see."

An hour later the home phone rang. Eileen picked it up, wondering why Larry hadn't called her cell phone instead.

"Good evening." The voice sounded husky, male and somewhat familiar. "May I speak with Miss Alfreda?"

Eileen blinked, confused. "Who's this?"

The man on the other end gave a slight chuckle. "Oh dear. This is Edwin Pryce. Miss Alfreda is expecting my call." The British accent rang a bell.

Eileen's eyes flared in surprise. "Ah! You're the butler from Winchester Manor."

"Yes. I started a week ago, along with all the newly hired house staff. I do hope it's acceptable that I've called."

She didn't know what to say, so she passed Alfie the phone. "It's Edwin, the Winchesters' butler—for you."

With a small gasp, Alfie grabbed the phone. Like an excited schoolgirl, she disappeared into her bedroom.

Zoe giggled. "Alfie's got a man. Whoo-oo!"

"Shh! She might hear you."

"You know, they were really cute

together. I've never seen Alfie laugh so much. Do you think he's asking her out?"

"I'm thinking this is none of our business. And no teasing her."

Zoe skipped into the living room and plopped down on the sofa. "I think it's sweet."

Eileen had to agree. Finding a love interest so late in life *was* sweet—and it wasn't easy. She should know. She'd been single ever since her divorce from Frank, and the past five years had whizzed by. To be honest, Eileen didn't have the time or the energy to commit to dating anyone. But she did miss the intimacy.

She headed for her office, picked up the phone and dialed Rick Martin's number. When he answered, she filled him in on the missing money.

"You did good."

"Try not to sound so surprised."

"Nothing you do surprises me."

Martin's comment caught her off guard, and she floundered for words, "I, uh…"

"I emailed you a copy of the security footage and guest list."

She blew out a breath. "You find anything?"

"Nothing that stands out. Maybe you'll

have better luck. Let's connect tomorrow sometime."

"Sounds good. Night, Martin."

"Uh…one last thing…"

"Yeah?"

"None of this last name crap. The name's Rick."

Eileen stared at the receiver for a second. "Okay."

"We'll find the missing sister. Sleep well, Eileen."

"You too…*Rick.*"

Eileen hung up, her stomach twisting into a tight knot. She had a bad feeling that Vivian Winchester wasn't just missing. Somewhere out there was a body to go with all the blood. She prayed the woman was still breathing.

Chapter Seven

The following morning, Eileen sipped a Chai tea at the kitchen island, while Alfie and Zoe studied the copy of Walter Winchester's will in the dining room. As the elderly woman attempted to explain some of the terminology, Zoe made notes in the margins. Occasionally, the kid would look up something on her cell phone.

"I'm going to my office," Eileen told them. They barely acknowledged her.

A whiteboard in the far corner of the converted garage held photographs and other notes on her last case, a stolen ruby necklace. That case had been closed two days ago, after she'd photographed the thief at a Victoria nightclub. The victim's former best friend had stolen the necklace and blatantly showed it off to her new friends.

"Out with the old, and in with the new," Eileen muttered, sweeping everything from the board into a plastic container, which she labeled and stored on a top shelf in the closet.

Behind her, Zoe said, "Need any help?"

"Sure. Think you can take some notes for me on the computer?"

Eileen wasn't the most technologically astute. Truth be told, computers scared her. She'd probably push the wrong button and the damn thing would explode. Zoe had once told her that Exploding Computer Paranoia, or ECP, was a casualty of Eileen's generation. Hell, Zoe knew more about computers than she did.

"What do we know so far?" Eileen asked.

"A lady is missing," Zoe replied. "Something happened to her in those woods."

Eileen nodded. "Someone attacked her in the woods. Why?"

"Why do people hurt others?"

"For love, money, vengeance—too many motives to list."

"You said some money was missing. So…who needed it? I thought these people were rich."

"They are," Eileen said.

"Maybe they were desperate?"

Eileen eyed the whiteboard. Picking up a dry-erase marker, she wrote the two sisters' names at the top. Beside this, she added Chip Mulligan's name. The man had spent a lot of time with Vivian, and probably not just at Eagle Ridge. She made a note to check motels in the area around the golf course. Perhaps Vivian and Mulligan had hit more than *golf* balls.

Next, she added Patricia Carmo's name to the suspect list, though her gut told her the woman couldn't have harmed Vivian. Beside the lawyer's name, she wrote: *Johnny Blake / Ex?*

Her cell phone rang.

"Eileen? It's Rick."

"Good news or bad?"

"Both. What do you want first?"

"Give me the bad."

"Vivian Winchester's ex-husband is a bust. Blake's moved on, hasn't seen Vivian in over a year."

"I don't have much either," she admitted, erasing Johnny's name from the whiteboard. "I spoke with Vivian's golf instructor. He's definitely a ladies' man, but I don't see a motive."

"Who's the instructor?"

She gave him Chip Mulligan's name and waited for his reaction.

"Are you kidding me?" Martin made a sound that could have been a chuckle, or perhaps he was choking on a donut. Eileen wasn't sure.

"Nope. No joke."

"Okay. I'll look into Mulligan, see if he has a rap sheet."

"And the good news?"

"It's subjective. The DNA you collected at Eagle Ridge is a conclusive match to Vivian Winchester."

"So, she has officially moved from missing person to victim."

"Sadly, yes. We have an APB out on her, news stations will be briefed in an hour, and we've blasted all social networks with Vivian's photo."

"I'd like to be the one to tell her sister."

"Have at it. Certainly not my favorite part of the job, and I have a possible lead to follow anyway."

"Lead?"

"A vet clinic in Burnaby reported a

missing order of ketamine. I'll let you know if it pans out."

Eileen hung up. Returning to the dining room, she gave Alfie and Zoe a wave as she grabbed her jacket. "I'm heading out."

An hour later, Bored Guy buzzed Eileen through Winchester Manor's gates. As she parked the dilapidated Honda, she noticed a familiar black sedan parked around the side. The woman of the house was home.

When the front door opened, Edwin greeted her with a broad smile. "Miss Valerie is having a morning swim."

He led her through the house then outside to a heated saltwater oasis surrounded by gray and beige slabs of granite. A waterfall cascaded over a rocky edge at the far end, emphasized by blue lights woven between the boulders.

Treading water near the falls, Valerie Winchester smoothed her sleek black hair and smiled when she saw Eileen. "Miss Edwards!" She waved, swam the length of the pool then headed for the steps, her strappy neon-pink bikini leaving nothing to the imagination.

"Have a seat," Valerie said, slipping into a floral-printed silk robe that had been flung over a chaise lounge. "Edwin, can you bring us some ice tea?"

After the butler left, Eileen said, "I'm not here with good news."

Valerie's smile vanished. "Vivian's dead, isn't she?"

"We don't know that. What we do know is that police matched the DNA from Vivian's toothbrush to the blood found at Eagle Ridge. DNA on the scarf is also a match. There's no question that something happened to your sister in those woods."

"But Vivian could still be alive."

"Quite possibly. However, your sister has lost a lot of blood, and she hasn't been admitted to any hospital or clinic. If she is injured and doesn't get help soon…"

Valerie gave a sad nod. "I can finish that sentence. But I still don't understand why anyone would hurt Vivian."

Edwin approached them, a cordless phone in hand. "My apologies, Miss Valerie, but there's a gentleman on the home line who won't leave his name. He says it's urgent."

Valerie's eyes widened. "Maybe the police have found Vivian." She reached for the phone. "Hello? Who is this?"

Eileen couldn't hear what was being said

on the other end, but she could read the shock on Valerie's pale face as the woman listened to the caller.

"You want how much?" Valerie gasped and covered the receiver. "He's demanding three million dollars for Vivian's safe return."

Without a word, Eileen retrieved her cell phone and called Rick Martin. "You're running a tap on the Winchester home line, right?"

"Yeah, why?"

"Valerie is talking to a man right now who claims to have her sister."

"How much?"

"Three million." She heard Martin suck in a breath. "I'm listening to Valerie's end of the conversation."

"Have her put the call on speakerphone."

"We need to hear," Eileen whispered to Valerie.

Standing, the woman set the phone in the middle of the table and activated speakerphone mode. To the blackmailer, she said, "It's going to take me a few days to get that amount—"

"Don't give me that crap!"

The altered voice made it impossible to

confirm gender, age or accent.

"You have twenty-four hours. I'll call you tomorrow morning with further instructions."

"Wait!" Valerie shouted. "I need to know my sister's all right."

"She's tied up at the moment...pun intended. Twenty-four hours, or your sister's gonna lose more than a little blood." The call disconnected.

Valerie paced beside the table. "Oh my God, Vivian..."

"Ms. Winchester, you should sit down." To Martin, Eileen said, "He wasn't on long enough, was he?"

"No. Next time we need to keep him talking."

"And demand," she turned away from Valerie and lowered her voice, "proof of life."

"Exactly. Now that we know this is a hostage situation, I'll have Luis set up at the Manor. He can walk the sister through tomorrow's call. I'll have a team ready to stakeout the drop zone. Call me later tonight."

"Will do. Thanks, Rick."

"Good work, Eileen."

"I just happened to be here at the right

time."

"Then you have great timing." Martin's voice brightened, almost as if he were smiling.

Hanging up, she turned to Valerie. "An officer is on his way. He's going to monitor and record all incoming calls."

"But what if Vivian's captor gets spooked? What if he—"

"We can't go there. No more what-ifs. We know what he wants now, and that's a huge advantage."

"So, I pay him and get my sister back, and what—he goes free?"

"Don't worry about the details. Constable Luis Cayolla is on his way here, and he'll be able to tell you more. Of course, we're assuming that coming up with three million dollars won't be an issue for you."

"I'll call Patricia right away and have her release the funds." Valerie headed for the patio doors. "Are you staying until the police officer gets here?"

"I have somewhere I need to be. Sorry."

Valerie dabbed at the corner of her eyes with the sleeve of the robe. "I can't believe this is happening." A sob caught in the back of her throat. "My sister is everything to me."

"If all goes well, your sister will be home, safe and sound, tomorrow night."

"But what if it *doesn't* go well?"

Eileen reached out and patted the woman's arm. "Let's not go there. You need to stay positive."

She left Valerie staring off into space. She prayed the woman would hold things together and not go and do something stupid. Zoe's words echoed in her head. Maybe the kid was right. Maybe whoever took Vivian was desperate.

Desperate people do desperate things.

Sitting in her car in the driveway, Eileen used her new cell phone to search for motels and inns in close proximity to Eagle Ridge Golf & Country Club. The first on the list, Twin Pines Motel, offered rooms by the hour and wasn't in the best part of the city.

The front desk attendant shook his bald head when Eileen showed him the photos of Vivian and Mulligan twenty minutes later.

"My clientele is more low income, including johns and hookers," he said.

The next two motels produced the same results, so she aimed for mid-range hotels, of which there were two near the golf course.

The Mandarin Hotel was most frequented by business people, according to the fresh-faced Asian kid behind the front desk, who eyed her private investigator's ID with suspicion.

Eileen set the photos on the desk and slid them toward the clerk. "Have either of these people checked in to your hotel within the past month?"

"You got names?"

"Vivian Winchester and Chip Mulligan."

The kid punched the names into the computer in front of him. "Mr. Mulligan is here all the time, but I don't know his guests. Last time he was here was over two months ago." He scrunched his face as he peered closer at the photo of Vivian. "This lady, she looks kinda familiar…"

Eileen held her breath.

"Uh…no." He slid the photographs toward her. "I can't say for sure that she's been here. And I don't think I've seen her with that Mulligan guy. Sorry."

The second stop on Eileen's list: Coastal Waters Inn. This time the desk attendant was female, early forties, petite build. The instant the woman saw the photograph of Mulligan, she let out a small squeal. "I knew that man was trouble."

"Why do you say that?"

"Well, he rarely ever checks in with the same woman. Is he cheating on his wife?"

"I can't say. What about the woman in this photo? You see her here?"

"She doesn't look familiar. What's her name?"

"Vivian Winchester."

"She's not in our system, but I'm only the day manager. You should talk to the night manager. He's on at six."

"When was the last time Chip Mulligan was here?"

Clickety-clack went the computer keys. Seconds later, the woman looked up from the monitor and smiled. "Mr. Mulligan is checked in until tomorrow morning, but I don't think he's in his room right now. He usually heads out after breakfast."

Eileen slid a twenty-dollar bill across the desk. "Room number?"

The woman didn't miss a beat, sweeping the money into her jacket pocket. "Room 314. Hold on…" She reached beneath the counter. "I'm not really supposed to do this without a search warrant, but you look trustworthy, so here's a spare key. Please return it to me when you're done."

Eileen rode the elevator, uninterrupted, to the third floor. She paused in front of room 314 and scoped the hallway. *No witnesses. Good.*

She rapped twice on the door, unsure of what she'd say if Mulligan answered. A glance over one shoulder told her the hall was still empty. She pressed her ear against the wood.

Silence.

She knocked again. "House cleaning."

When no one came to the door, Eileen heaved a sigh of relief. The key card slid into the slot below the handle, and the door opened with a faint click. The hotel room wasn't anything spectacular, certainly not the kind of room a wealthy socialite would pay for. Somehow, she couldn't see Vivian Winchester here, not if she were anything like her sister.

Eileen headed for the king-sized bed first and gingerly peeled back the covers. She withdrew swabs and evidence tape packages from the inside pocket of her jacket and set them on the nightstand. She pressed the tape against the bedding in several places then slid the tape into its protective covering.

Frowning, she peeked in the drawers.

They were empty, except for the Bible in the left nightstand. Eileen didn't see Mulligan as a religious man, but she rifled through the pages, just in case they held a clue. They didn't.

"Clueless in Vancouver," she muttered.

After she rearranged the bedding, she headed for the closet, where she found a couple of t-shirts, a club jacket and a golf cap, all with the familiar Eagle Ridge logo. These were the only articles of clothing in the room.

Eileen used the swabs on the bathroom taps. She considered taking fingerprints, even though Vivian's weren't in the system. But if the woman had been one of Mulligan's latest conquests, her DNA would be all over the bed and bathroom.

Eileen's frown deepened. *Nothing in this room seems out of the ordinary.*

Chapter Eight

A quick Google search on her cell phone gave Eileen the address to Chip Mulligan's home, a small two-bedroom split level in Burnaby. Public records confirmed the house had originally belonged to his parents, who had retired and moved to Mexico two years ago.

Eileen glanced at her watch. 2:23 p.m. *Chip should be at Eagle Ridge, working his shift.*

She drove past the residence three times to determine if anyone was home, but the house remained cloaked in shadows and nothing moved within. She pulled up to the curb a few houses away, parked and climbed out. The burgundy front door beckoned, but she hesitated. Rick had said nothing about searching Mulligan's house. VPD didn't have enough evidence to get a judge to sign off on a search warrant.

Then again, Eileen was no longer a member of VPD.

As she strode toward the house, the next-door neighbor opened his door. The elderly man wore a dingy, coffee-stained housecoat. With bare feet and legs, he stepped outside then trudged toward the newspaper abandoned at the bottom of the steps. He didn't notice Eileen until he turned back.

"You look too old to be one of Chip's whores," the man muttered.

"You look too old to be outside with bare feet," Eileen shot back.

The man gave her a lecherous grin. "It's not just my feet that're bare. Wanna see?" He reached for the loose knot he'd tied to one side of the housecoat.

"You do that, and I'll have to call the cops." She thrust her ID in his face.

The old man scowled. "Aw, you're no fun, Madam Investigator."

"If it's fun you want, maybe you could help me with something." She showed him

Vivian's photo. "Ever see this woman visiting Mr. Mulligan?"

"Can't say that I have. Then again, Chip changes women more than he washes that truck of his at that golf course he works at—and that's a hell of a lot."

"You live here long?"

"Over twenty years. I moved here after the Mulligans bought their house."

"You know them well?"

He shrugged. "Well enough to know their son is a good-for-nothing lazy-ass. Dirk never should've given Chip that house." He spat in the direction of the Mulligan home. "Kid has zero respect for property, much less for women."

"Thank you for your time, Mr…"

"Picard. Gerald Picard. And you are?"

"I was never here, Mr. Picard."

He grinned and winked. "I get you. I never saw you."

"Saw who?" She gave him a nod. "Thank you, Mr. Picard."

After the elderly man disappeared inside his home, Eileen made a beeline for the single garage at the back end of Chip Mulligan's property. She peered through the grimy window. The empty garage made sense since Mulligan should be at Eagle

Ridge. A digital-coded lock on the side door to the garage presented the only challenge. On a lark, she punched in 1111 and snorted out loud when the lock clicked open. Some people were so lazy.

The small garage hoarded a typical mix of grimy tools and automotive products and parts, proof that a man reigned supreme here. A pair of dingy gray overalls hung from a hook near the door. She checked the pockets, but they were empty. A thorough search of toolboxes and shelves confirmed the garage was a dead end.

Next, Eileen scurried around the side of Mulligan's house and peered into a kitchen window. Dirty dishes in the sink and empty pizza boxes on a cluttered dining room table revealed that Mulligan used his parents' former home as his "man cave." She highly doubted Vivian Winchester had ever set foot in the place.

She moved stealthily around to the back deck and pushed on the sliding door. She sucked in a breath when it popped open. Mulligan clearly felt safe in his neighborhood if he didn't bother locking his doors.

"An open door is an invitation," she muttered.

Taking a deep breath, she stepped inside and closed the sliding door. A clock ticked ominously somewhere in the house. A search of the kitchen yielded nothing suspicious, so she made her way into the living room. She carefully lifted the sofa cushions and checked the drawers of an old desk. She found an outdated calendar and flipped through the pages. Nothing there either.

With a nervous glance over one shoulder, she headed upstairs. Partway up, she discovered an antique pendulum clock anchored to the wall of the landing.

Tick, tick, tick...

The first door led to the bathroom.

Eileen rifled through drawers and the medicine cabinet but came up empty. The second door turned out to be Mulligan's bedroom. Searching under the bed, behind a bookshelf and in the closet revealed nothing out of the ordinary. She peeled back the comforter and inspected the sheets and pillows. Nothing. Not one speck of hair or smudge of makeup. Eileen doubted whether *any* female had ever been in Mulligan's bed—or bedroom.

Discouraged, she let out a sigh and eyed the last door. *Office?*

She pushed the door open and gaped in utter shock. "What the hell?" Her cheeks burned. "Fifty shades of *Ew!*"

Vertical blinds in the burgundy room blocked most light. However, a scented wax warmer glowed a few feet away, illuminating enough of the space that she could see a wide assortment of sex toys, blindfolds, whips, feathers, chains and other sexual gear hanging on the walls. A black leather swing hung from heavy-duty steel hooks in the ceiling.

"No under-ducks for Mr. Mulligan," she murmured dryly.

She hurried downstairs. The basement door opened off the kitchen, and she'd left it for last on purpose. Basements were her least favorite area of a home, especially in older neighborhoods where they tended to be cold, raw and unfinished.

She flicked the switch at the top step. Down below, a light flickered twice. With a fortifying breath, she strode down the stairs. The center of the basement was set up as an exercise room. Mulligan had invested in a universal weight machine, a treadmill and a rowing machine. Multiple sets of round weights, from ten to fifty pounds, rested on the floor. An old television sat on a small table across from the treadmill. The exercise area was the cleanest part of the house. Not a speck of dust anywhere.

Eileen pondered this for a moment. Mulligan was down here regularly, and he was in perfect shape and had the strength to take down a grown woman who was also in peak condition. But where would he hide her?

Concrete walls displayed a variety of wooden shelves and glass jars filled with fruits, vegetables and God knows what—all dated over ten years ago. The only door in the basement led to a utility room. The furnace barely fit inside, much less a grown woman.

Eileen skimmed both hands along the walls, praying for signs of a secret room. A thud resounded overhead. She froze.

Footsteps...

Someone was in the house.

Ah, shit...he's home!

What would Mulligan do if he found her trespassing? He'd be pissed and probably call the cops. Last thing she needed was Larry breathing down her neck about following proper protocol.

Footsteps plodded overhead.

Panic rose in her chest, and she

struggled to bring her racing pulse under control as she flicked off the basement light and ducked behind a cardboard wardrobe box.

Upstairs, footsteps were followed by soft thuds.

She clamped her lips shut. *Please don't come down...*

The door at the top of the stairs creaked open.

Eileen huddled lower, cloaked by distorted shadows. Could he hear her breathing? Reaching for her gun, she bit back a groan. *Damn! Left it at home.*

A figure in an oversized hoodie hovered on the top step. The combination of dim light and the hood made it impossible to identify the culprit.

Eileen considered her options. She could come forward, explain her reason for being there and hope that Mulligan felt generous, or she could remain where she was and wait for him to leave. She chose the latter.

The hooded figure turned away, closed the basement door and paced around the main floor for fifteen minutes before Eileen heard a door slam. She waited another ten minutes to be sure.

When the house was finally still, she

made her way back upstairs.

Overall, nothing indicated the hooded person had disturbed anything in the house—until Eileen caught sight of an open closet door.

I shut that...

Dread slithered up her spine. Was he hiding in the closet, ready to lunge and attack her?

She moved toward it, one hand stretched toward the knob, but before she reached it, the closet door flew open. A rush of stale air and dark fabric breezed over her as someone tackled her to the floor. The weight was almost suffocating. She wriggled away, desperate to put space between her and her attacker.

"Get off me!"

"Eileen?" a familiar voice said.

Chapter Nine

Eileen stared up at Rick Martin, who lay stretched out on top of her, his hands gripping her wrists, pinning her to the floor. Their eyes met, and she saw fury in his.

"You can let me up now, Rick."

"Jesus, Eileen…" He jumped to his feet and held out a hand. "I thought you were an intruder."

She took his hand, and he helped her to her feet. "I thought *you* were the intruder."

"I-I could've really hurt you."

She rubbed her wrists. "Forget about it."

With a tortured expression in his eyes, he took her hand and studied the red marks he'd left on her wrist. "I'm so sorry.

I…uh…"

"I'm tough, remember?" She forced a laugh, lost in the sensation of his warn fingers stroking her skin. She shivered and pulled away.

For the first time in years, Eileen was at a loss for words.

Rick gritted his teeth. "What are you doing here? We don't have a warrant yet."

"I could ask you the same thing. You must've heard someone calling for help?" She grinned at him, determined to erase the guilty look from his face.

He stared at her then cocked his head to one side. "That's my story. And here you are, needing some rescuing."

"Rescuing? I was doing quite fine on my own, thank you."

"So, no sign of Vivian Winchester?"

She shook her head. "No secret rooms, no visible blood, nothing suspicious except you." In the dim light, she studied him for a second. Then she gasped. "Wait! You're not wearing a hoodie."

Rick's brow furrowed. "No…"

"Someone else *was* here!"

"What?"

"I was in the basement a few minutes ago. Then I heard footsteps, and someone wearing a dark hoodie came down the basement stairs, just a few steps."

Rick's gaze hardened. "That wasn't me." He strode to the living room window. "No movement outside. Whoever it was, he's long gone."

She pulled her cell phone from her pocket.

"Who you calling, Eileen?"

"Eagle Ridge." To the woman who answered, Eileen said, "Can you tell me if Chip Mulligan is on the course right now?" She listened for a moment, thanked her and hung up, more confused than ever.

"Is he there?" Rick asked.

"Yeah, since noon."

"So, we know Chip wasn't the person you saw."

"And I doubt it was a random break and enter. The timing is too coincidental."

"Description?"

"Medium height, medium build, jeans and hoodie." She shrugged. "Too dark to tell if male or female."

"In other words, we've got—"

"A big, whoppin' nada."

Rick checked his watch. "It's almost three. Have you eaten yet?"

"No…"

He steered her toward the back door. "Let's grab a bite. There's a Boston Pizza about three blocks away. Meet you there."

Eileen parked her battered car next to Rick's sparkling silver Ford Edge. Flipping the visor down, she glanced at her reflection. "Okay, Eileen, it's been a while since you've shared a meal with a man. Try not to slop on your clothes or spit food at him."

She entered the restaurant and spotted Rick seated near a window. He waved and smiled—a real smile this time. She'd broken through his stiff façade.

"I'm growing on you, aren't I?" she teased.

"Larry said you were one of the best cops he's ever known."

"Well, I'll warn you, he's a bit biased. We've been friends a long time."

"He never told me why you left."

She bit her bottom lip. "It's a long story. Maybe another time."

He nodded. "I get it. Too personal."

"Too painful." She inadvertently rubbed the small scar on her right hand.

A young man approached and took their orders. After he left, Eileen said, "I have some evidence samples." She reached into her jacket and retrieved the swab and tape bags and handed them to Rick.

"I'll have the lab get on these ASAP."

"I did find something unusual at Chip's," she said after a moment. "He's got a sex room upstairs filled with…um…whips and ropes."

Rick arched a brow. "You're joking."

"Not one bit."

He threw back his head and laughed. "Sorry, I'm imagining your face when you opened the door."

"Hey, I'm no prude. I've seen worse on the job."

"But this was your first sex room?"

"Yup. With a bed and a leather swing and dozens of…um…devices."

"Isn't that what we all have?"

"Yeah, and stripper poles." She chuckled. "That's the only thing missing."

"Except for Vivian Winchester," he reminded her.

Their meals arrived, and they ate in silence, each deep in thought. Eileen had ordered a salad loaded with crispy chicken and cheese. She spent most of her time glaring at the juicy burger Rick devoured.

"You've got mayonnaise on your chin," she blurted.

Rick reached for a napkin but missed the spot entirely. "The burgers here are messy but sublime."

She resisted the urge to lean forward and wipe the mayo from the corner of his mouth, an act that would be far too intimate. Instead, she pushed her plate aside and groaned. "I'm stuffed."

"Don't know how that's possible. You haven't finished your salad."

"Full is full," she said, a phrase her father used to say.

Rick leaned forward, a fork poised in one hand. He speared a chunk of chicken from her plate and popped it into his mouth. "If you're not going to finish that…"

She slid her plate toward him. "Have at it."

Rick Martin intrigued her. When she'd first met him, he'd seemed standoffish. Now, not so much. Quite the conundrum.

"Larry told me about your son," Rick said quietly. "That must've been difficult for you and your husband."

"It was. But time heals."

"That's what they say."

"It's the truth. With life comes death. It's part of the package deal we all get."

He covered her hand with his warm

palm. "No parent should outlive their children. It's not right."

"Neither is having your kids whisked away to Winnipeg." She slowly extricated her hand from his. "Sorry."

"Ah, so Larry told you."

She shrugged. "I like to know who I'm working with."

"I can be a bit of a—"

"Yes?" She grinned.

"I'll let you fill in the blank, once you've made up your mind about me."

"Maybe I already have."

He stared intensely. "Not yet. But you will."

She found a twenty-dollar bill in her jacket pocket and set it on the table.

Rick pushed the twenty toward her. "*My* treat."

"I can pay for my own lunch."

"I know you can, but I insist."

She wasn't sure if he was being chivalrous or if he simply wanted the write-off, but either way she tucked the money back into her pocket. "Thank you."

"You can buy next time."

His comment unnerved her. *Next time? Would there be a next time?*

The real question was whether she

wanted there to be a next time.

Before she could reply, they were interrupted by a short, squat man in his late forties. "Hey, Martin! You gonna eat everything at the table?"

Rick's expression darkened. "How'd you find me?"

The stranger let out a gruff laugh. "Saw your SUV in the parking lot." Black eyes rimmed by silver-framed eyeglasses stared down at her. "You must be Eileen Edwards, the PI." The man held out a hand. "Luis Cayolla, VPD."

"Ah, Rick's partner," Eileen said with a nod.

She watched the uneasy comradery between the two men. Cayolla had an outgoing, humorous personality, while Rick was still learning to trust again. The two men were as opposite as day and night, but when it came to the investigation, they were on the same page.

Cayolla caught her gaze. "Mexican-Canadian."

Eileen blinked. "Pardon?"

"You were contemplating my nationality. My parents were both born in Juarez, Mexico, but immigrated to Canada almost fifty years ago. I was born here."

"Lucky you." Being Canadian was always something she was proud of.

"Now that we've got that out of the way…" Cayolla gave her a wink and slipped into the seat beside her. "You know the service road for landscapers and the greenskeeper?" He consulted his cell phone. "It was used last Tuesday night to transport a couple of large boulders to the sixteenth hole. I already questioned the greenskeeper, Fred Zimmerman. He saw nothing out of the ordinary."

Eileen and Rick filled Cayolla in on their search of Mulligan's house and the enigmatic intruder wearing a hoodie.

"And *you* never saw who it was?" Cayolla asked Rick.

"No, and I'm not getting a good feeling," Rick muttered.

Eileen sighed. "Me neither. Whoever it was, they were skulking around Mulligan's house. Why?"

"That's the question of the day," Rick said.

"Could be completely unrelated to our case," Cayolla offered.

Rick shrugged. "Maybe."

A question crept into Eileen's mind. *What if Mulligan has a partner?*

At 5:50 p.m., Eileen pulled into the driveway and noticed a ten-speed bicycle leaning against her house. A skull-decorated skateboard sat propped up against the back tire of the bike. Zoe had a visitor. *Spence.*

Eileen had mixed feelings about the kid. Spence was a couple years older than Zoe, whom he'd known as "Zipper" when she'd lived as a boy on the street, and he had more glittery bling on his face than Eileen had in her jewelry box. Then there was the makeup—black eyeliner, blue mascara and sometimes black lipstick. Goth? Emo? Gay? Eileen didn't know which, but it made her nervous.

She entered via the office door and dropped her jacket and keys on the desk.

Alfie had left a sticky note on the computer monitor. *Gone to dinner and a movie with E. Don't wait up!* It was signed with a capital *A.*

Eileen sighed. "Have fun, Alfie." *Hell, someone should.*

When she entered the house, she found Zoe and Spence at the dining room table, Zoe's laptop sat open and their heads nearly touched. They jumped back, guilt written all over their faces.

"What's up?" Eileen asked, eyes narrowing.

"Nothing," the teens chimed in unison.

She prayed they weren't watching porn. "Movie?"

Zoe looked at Spence. "Not exactly…"

"Don't blame Zipper," Spence said, pushing a blue streak of hair away from his kohl-lined eyes. "I told her I'd help."

"Help with what?"

Zoe gave her a small smile and held out her hand. "The flash drive with the golf course's security videos."

"That video is part of a police investigation. I don't think you—"

"But Spence found something."

That had Eileen's attention.

"Rewind the video," Zoe told Spence. To Eileen, she said, "I wrote the date and time down so you'd find it easier."

Eileen reached for the note and skimmed the information. Spence and Zoe had discovered a figure entering the main lobby via a side door at 2:30 a.m. on a Monday morning a week earlier.

As the video reached the correct timeframe, the camera revealed a man wearing a club jacket and cap, but murky night lights hid the person's identity, even when he paused near the door to the men's locker room.

Zoe tapped the monitor. "Freeze it there!"

"Weird time to be playing golf," Spence said.

"Zoom in on the name tag on his jacket," Zoe said eagerly.

Spence did so, and Eileen blew out a breath. "Gotcha!"

The camera clearly showed a man entering the men's locker room.

She punched in Rick's number on her cell phone. When he answered, she said, "You can pursue that warrant now for a *legal* search of Chip Mulligan's residence *and* club locker. We've got probable cause. It's on the video."

She told him what Zoe had found, though she intentionally left out Spence's involvement. Rick hung up, promising to get the warrant, while Eileen's mind whirled with questions. Two people were involved in Vivian's abduction. That much was clear. *Mulligan and...?*

She let out a sudden gasp. *What if Vivian and Mulligan had faked the kidnapping for the money?* That might explain the disorganization of the kidnappers, the late ransom call and the lack of a body.

Unless Mulligan becomes desperate.

Chapter Ten

While Alfie and Zoe slept in the following morning, Eileen woke early, thrilled by the possibility that Vivian Winchester would be found and brought home to her sister. Some days her work seemed more rewarding than others. She prayed this would be one of them.

While making a cup of Chai tea in the kitchen, she checked her cell phone and discovered she'd missed a call. Rick had left a text message.

Meet me at Winchester Manor at 8 a.m.

"Yes, sir."

Winchester   Manor   appeared

inconspicuous on the outside. The bare driveway suggested there were no visitors. Inside, however, was another story. Two female rookies strode through the house, checking windows and doors. A third uniformed officer she recognized— Constable Antoniuk, from the crime scene. He waved her through the house.

"Nothing yet," Luis Cayolla said when she found him in the study. Valerie Winchester sat beside him, impatient fingers tapping the desktop.

Eileen nodded. "We all ready?"

"Ready as we'll ever be," Cayolla said, pulling her aside and lowering his voice. "By the way, Rick's got a tail on that golf instructor. If Mulligan makes the ransom call, or makes an appearance to pick up the money, we'll take him down."

Eileen checked her watch. Thirty minutes to go.

Valerie rose gracefully. "Does anyone want tea or coffee?" Without waiting for a reply, she left the study.

"Is Valerie okay?" Eileen frowned. "She seems really preoccupied."

"She's worried something'll go wrong at the drop," Cayolla replied.

And it might. Eileen knew, firsthand,

how badly ransom drops could go.

The phone rang, and everyone froze.

Somewhere in the house, Valerie picked up. So did Cayolla. After a few seconds, he sighed and removed his headphones. "The gardener is sick and won't be here today."

Eileen blew out a pent-up breath.

Valerie returned to the study with a navy-blue duffel bag. She dropped it on the floor. *Thud!*

"The payoff?" Eileen asked.

Valerie nodded. "Cash weighs a ton. I'm more of a Visa kind of gal." She let out a shaky laugh. "Edwin is making coffee and tea for us, and there's an assortment of fresh-baked muffins, breads and fruit in the dining room. Help yourself any time."

"Thank you." Eileen patted the woman's shoulder. "I know you're scared, but Constable Martin and his team will do everything to bring your sister home."

"I just pray she's not seriously hurt."

Eileen considered the amount of blood—and the tooth—found at the crime scene. Had the tooth been extracted while Vivian was conscious, or after she'd been drugged with ketamine? Or had the blood come from another wound? At least now that there'd been a ransom demand, the kidnapper would have to keep Vivian alive.

A shrill ring cut through the silence.

Valerie slumped into the chair, her face pale and her hands clenched into fists. Drawing in a deep breath, she gave a nod to Cayolla beside her. He tapped his laptop and activated the speakerphone.

"Winchester residence," Valerie said.

"Got the money?" the digitally-altered voice asked.

"Yes. Three million."

Cayolla shoved a note toward Valerie. *Get proof of life!*

"I want to talk to my sister. I need to know she's okay."

"You know the rules. She can't talk, but I can show her to you." The voice gave her a website address, and she wrote it on the note Cayolla had given her.

Eileen moved behind Cayolla, peering over his shoulder at the monitor.

A moment later, a live camera feed showed a barely recognizable Vivian Winchester tied to a chair, her mouth covered with a strip of electrical tape. She wore baggy track pants, an oversized sweatshirt and a bloody towel around her head.

Cayolla zoomed in on Vivian's face.

Bruises and lacerations covered the woman's left cheek, her eye swollen and half-closed

"Oh God..." Valerie moaned. "What did you do to her?"

"We had a...little altercation," the voice said. "She's fine though."

In the background, Vivian struggled to escape. Her mouth moved frantically behind the tape, but all they heard were shrieks and grunts.

"Okay, that's enough," the voice commanded.

The live feed disappeared, despite Cayolla's attempts to refresh the website.

"Bring the money to Granville Island. Come alone. No police. There's a public payphone near The Oyster Shack. I'll call you in one hour."

"Wait!" Valerie cried out. "When will I get my sister?"

"When I've got the money." The line went dead.

"I'll review the video," Cayolla said to Eileen. "Martin wants you to accompany Ms. Winchester to the drop zone, but stay incognito."

"Who else will be there?"

"Constables Martin and Norman plus a

couple of undercovers. They'll take care of whoever shows up for the money. Your job will be to ensure Valerie Winchester's safety."

"Don't worry," Eileen said, glancing at Valerie, "I won't let anything happen to you."

"That's reassuring."

Eileen couldn't tell if the comment was sincere or not.

"I'll have my driver pull the car around front." Valerie stood. "Bring the bag, won't you?" She left before Eileen or Cayolla could reply.

Eileen reached for the bag, hefted it off the floor and grunted her displeasure. The last time she'd lifted something *that* heavy, she'd hauled a body out of a drainage pipe. An elderly man with dementia had crawled inside to escape Mother Nature's downpour. No one knew for sure how long he'd been in the pipe, but by the time Eileen found him, his body had bloated to nearly twice its size. Not a pretty sight.

"Hold on, Ms. Edwards." Cayolla jumped to his feet. "I'll take the bag to the car."

"I appreciate it. I'm afraid my weightlifting days are over."

She had to give Cayolla credit. For a small man, he didn't make a peep when she shoved the duffel bag into his waiting arms. She followed him to the front door, opened it for him and watched as he deposited the bag in the trunk of the black sedan.

Valerie exited the house and slid elegantly into the back seat. Eileen took the seat beside her with far less grace. Somehow, she'd managed to catch and tear one pant leg in the car door. As the driver pulled away, she sighed and made a mental note to buy new jeans.

She plucked her cell phone from her jacket and called Rick. "We're on our way to Granville Island."

"Great. We're already here."

"So, what's the plan?"

"We give him what he wants, and with any luck we get the sister back in one piece."

"What if he doesn't bring her? He said Valerie would get Vivian *after* he got the money."

"If he doesn't bring her, we'll follow him when he leaves."

"Of course, the abductor could be female," she reminded him.

"Unlikely, but possible."

Eileen knew the stats. The majority of abductors were male. They had the strength needed to subdue their targets—especially in a heavily wooded area with rough groundcover. Vivian had been dragged through the woods. Then what? Loaded into a waiting vehicle? That made the most sense. And *that* would take strength.

Valerie yawned loudly. "Sorry…I haven't been sleeping well."

"That's totally understandable."

The woman twisted a strand of hair around her index finger. "You sure my microphone is on?"

"Yes." Eileen handed her an earbud. "Put this in your ear. If you need assistance, we can advise you on what to say."

Earlier, Cayolla had asked Eileen to wire Valerie with a concealed microphone, on the off-chance the abductor said something incriminating during the money drop. Even a hint of Vivian's location could be helpful.

"Remember, if he suspects he's being recorded, he may bolt," Eileen said. "Don't look for us, don't speak overly loud, and don't do anything to give him the impression that you're *not* alone."

Valerie nodded.

Eileen smiled. "We'll be there for you,

watching. And when Constable Martin determines the timing is right, we'll bring down everyone involved in abducting your sister."

Valerie visibly shivered. "I just want this to be over."

"Soon. You've got to have faith."

"Faith is difficult to have when someone else controls your life."

Eileen pondered Valerie's words. *She's right.   How   sad…*

Chapter Eleven

As the driver parked the sedan, Eileen stared out the window at the throngs of people meandering along the Granville Island boardwalk. False Creek was equally busy; the many water taxis transported people from one side of the river to the other.

"What's wrong?" Valerie asked, frowning.

"I'm thinking he picked the perfect place. It's public and busy." *And there are far too many ways for him to escape.*

Granville Island, a historical gem in the heart of Vancouver, catered to artists, foodies and tourists. Open from early morning until late evening, it offered a spectacular view and numerous food choices, including a market that sold fresh seafood harvested from the Pacific Ocean.

"You know what to do, Ms. Winchester?"

Valerie nodded. "I'll do my best." She fitted the tiny flesh-colored bud in her ear. "You sure he can't see this?"

"No one can. But you'll be able to hear Constable Martin." She nodded toward the door. "You first. I'll be following at a safe distance, along with the best of VPD."

Valerie opened the door and stepped outside. "Here goes."

Eileen pushed the bag of money toward her. "Do *not* give him the money until he has either brought your sister to the drop or told you where she is."

"Provided she's alive, you mean."

"I believe she is."

Valerie grabbed the duffel bag with both hands and headed toward the boardwalk. Eileen watched the woman struggle with the cumbersome bag to the Oyster Shack at the far end. Occasionally, she'd rest the bag on a bench for a few minutes then off she'd go again.

Eileen waited five minutes before

leaving the car. Wearing a floppy sun hat, dull jeans and a Disturbed t-shirt she'd found in Will's stuff, she looked less like a private investigator and more like an older woman with peculiar music tastes out for her daily walk and shopping excursion. She popped an earbud receiver in her ear and heard Rick talking softly to Valerie, telling her that he had her back.

Eileen remained several yards behind Valerie, surveying the crowds for a familiar face. She saw Rick standing near The Oyster Shack. Cayolla stood several yards farther down the boardwalk, while Dutch and Larry, who were dressed in jeans and t-shirts, played cards on a bench closer to Eileen. God only knew where the undercovers were, but they were here somewhere.

She watched Valerie approach the public payphone. A few minutes later, the phone rang, and the woman picked up. Via the microphone hidden under the collar of Valerie's blouse, Eileen overheard the conversation.

"Take the money to the water taxi by the marketplace," the altered voice said. The call ended abruptly.

Sudden motion caught Eileen's eye. Larry and Dutch had ditched the card game and were walking swiftly toward the marketplace. They passed Valerie without incident.

As police closed in on the water taxi area, Rick approached Eileen with caution. As he passed her, he said, "We'll take him before he boards. Wait here."

Eileen sat on a bench, her fingers nervously tapping the armrest. *Maybe it would've been wiser to follow the suspect rather than arrest him. Maybe he'd lead us to Vivian.*

From her vantage point, she could only see Valerie. Rick and the others had merged with the masses. She watched as Valerie paused again, hefting the duffel bag onto a picnic table in order to catch her breath.

"Keep walking," Eileen whispered. "Don't back out now."

Without warning, a sleek black motorcycle came out of nowhere, causing passersby to shout and dart out of its path. A slim form in full leather attire straddled the machine. The rider wore a black helmet, the visor completely obscuring his face. Hunched low, he raced toward the unsuspecting woman.

"Valerie!" Eileen shouted.

The rider's gloved hand swooped down

and plucked the duffel bag from the picnic table, nearly knocking Valerie over in the process. The motorcycle sped past Eileen and disappeared, merging into regular traffic.

"He got away, Rick!" she shouted into the handheld radio. "He's on a black Suzuki motorcycle."

"Did you get the license?"

"No plate." She frowned. "He set this up so that if Valerie alerted police, you'd be too busy with the water taxis to prevent his escape."

Dutch and Larry sprinted past her, heading for the parking lot. She watched them climb into their respective unmarked vehicles and speed off in pursuit.

"Did I mess things up?" Valerie asked as she drew near, a mix of fear and guilt in her eyes. "What happened? Where's my sister?"

"You did everything right. Detectives Norman and Ducci are following the suspect. All we can do is wait." The words sounded flat and uncomforting, even to Eileen.

"But he has the money now. What if he disappears and we never hear from him again? What happens to Vivian?"

"He may have planned to let your sister

go afterward. From what I've seen so far, this entire abduction has been sloppy at best." In fact, the whole operation looked fishy. Definitely not professionals looking to score big with the Winchester fortune.

Returning to the parking lot, Valerie and Eileen climbed into the back seat of the sedan. Eileen instructed the driver to take them back to Winchester Manor.

Valerie blinked back tears. "I don't know what I'll do if Vivian—"

"Don't go there. Speculating won't make things easier. Let's give the detectives time to see where this leads."

Eileen's cell phone buzzed. Rick had left her a text message: *Lost suspect. Tracker tossed.*

She released a heavy breath. *Damn...*

Leaving a distraught Valerie in the driveway of Winchester Manor, Eileen climbed into her car and headed for the nearest Starbucks for a Chai tea latte. She needed a boost of caffeine. Maybe it would clear her fuzzy mind and bring her some clarity.

As she waited in the drive-through lane, Eileen mulled over the morning's catastrophic events. Whoever had the duffel bag of money also had Vivian Winchester. Now there was no reason to keep the victim. At least, not alive.

She shivered with dread.

Nothing added up with this case. The suspect had been disorganized during the abduction, leaving evidence in plain sight, but he planned every detail of the money drop. Was this a plan hatched by college kids out for a lark? Even the cash amount was suspicious.

"Follow the money," she murmured, inching the car closer to the window.

The amount demanded by the abductor was miniscule in comparison to the total Winchester fortune. If a pro had come up with the idea, the Winchester fortune would've dwindled substantially. But if money wasn't the ultimate goal, what was?

She considered the facts of the case. Vivian Winchester had been attacked in the woods at Eagle Ridge and abducted. The video sent to her sister suggested the woman was alive, but what would the abductor do now? If Vivian could identify her attacker, she was a dead woman. But if whoever took her thought he could milk more money from her sister, maybe he'd keep Vivian alive—at least for a while longer. Maybe long enough for VPD to find her.

Eileen's cell phone rang. She'd long since given up on Bluetooth devices. They irritated her ears. Since there was no hands-free calling in her ancient Honda, she pulled over to the side of the road.

"We're stumped," Rick said, his voice exasperated and tired.

"Any word on Vivian?"

"No. We're running the Suzuki through the system, but without even a partial plate number, we could be wading through days of paperwork."

"What about Chip Mulligan?"

"Already checked. He doesn't own a motorcycle, and witnesses place him at Eagle Ridge all morning."

"Who the hell does that leave?"

"Your guess is as good as mine."

"What about the search warrant?"

"Judge says we don't have enough."

Shit. "I'm wondering if we've been looking at this all wrong."

"How do you mean?"

"Well, you *first* thought this was a professional abduction of a wealthy socialite, right? What if this was more personal than that?"

"Personal, how?"

"I'm not sure." She thought of Vivian, her face battered and bruised. "The brutality of her abduction leads me to believe this is personal. Maybe I'm grasping at straws, but I don't think money is the driving factor here. If it were, the kidnappers would've demanded more, and Vivian Winchester would be at home, having lunch with her sister."

"If you're right and this is personal, we might not see a good outcome."

"I have a hunch. I'm going to check it out. If it pays off, I'll call you."

"Where are you heading?"

Eileen glanced at the clock on the dashboard. "Back to Eagle Ridge. I feel like we're missing something."

She hastily grabbed the Chai tea when the attendant leaned out the window. She shoved a five dollar bill into the boy's hand. "Keep the change."

The Honda backfired as she sped off in search of answers.

Eagle Ridge Golf & Country Club bustled with members by the time Eileen arrived. She squeezed her car into the last spot available in the guest parking lot, opened the glovebox, grabbed a couple of evidence bags and stuffed them in her jacket pocket.

Leaving the car, she wandered around the lot, searching for a black Suzuki. Nothing. She veered toward the members parking lot. No motorcycle there either. The staff parking lot revealed two motorcycles, but one was an older banana-yellow Yamaha. The other was a pristine steel-blue Kawasaki.

"Hey, Madam Private Investigator!" a voice called out.

Eileen spun around. "Ah...Mr. Mulligan, what can I do for you?"

Chip Mulligan flashed his pearly whites. "Maybe it's what I can do for *you*."

His charm probably worked miracles on the socialites, but not on Eileen.

She gave him a wry smile. "A-ha! You *do* know something."

Mulligan's grin faded. "You're wasting your time on me. I don't have a clue where Vivian is. Last time I spoke with her, she was on a rampage about that sister of hers. In fact, she jokingly asked me if I knew a hitman."

"A hitman?" The pulse in Eileen's throat skipped a beat.

"Listen, I didn't want to get Viv in

trouble with police, so I didn't say anything before, but with everything that's happened now, I thought you should know. At the time, I seriously thought she was joking. You know how family can be."

"Yeah, you can't pick your family. At least not the one you're born into."

"But you *can* choose which ones you invest your time and energy into. One thing I guarantee, Valerie Winchester isn't all innocence and properness. Maybe she found out her sister wanted her out of the picture and decided to get to her first."

"Do you know if the Winchesters own a motorcycle?"

Mulligan snickered. "Not those women. They're either driving the latest luxury sedan or they're being driven around." He frowned. "What does a motorbike have to do with anything?"

"Do you own one?"

He shook his head. "I have a feeling you already know the answer to that question. I prefer to keep my skin intact."

Considering Mulligan was her main suspect, he seemed overly calm and collected. Then again, if he'd sent his partner to pick up the money, he'd be free to establish an alibi."

"Know anyone with a black Suzuki motorcycle?"

"Nope. Wish I could help, I really do." He leaned closer. "The rumor mill says there was a ransom demand. That true?"

"I'm not at liberty to discuss the details of an open investigation."

Mulligan shrugged. "I'm not the guy you're looking for." He chuckled and added in a monotone voice, *"These aren't the droids you're looking for."*

"Huh?"

"The famous line from Star Wars?" His brows arched when she made no comment. "Don't tell me you haven't seen Star Wars. Best movie ever! The original three are so much better than the sequels and prequels."

"Listen, I'm not here to discuss movies. I'm here on official—"

"Hey," he interrupted, holding up his hands in surrender, "I get that you've got a job to do, but I'm telling you, I'm not your guy."

"Then you've got nothing to worry about."

He threw her a cocky smirk. "Who says I'm worried?"

As she headed back to the clubhouse, she wondered about the hitman theory

Mulligan had proposed. Could Valerie Winchester have set the whole thing up? Had she hired someone to do the deed? Was she responsible for her sister's kidnapping? And did she intend to kill Vivian, her own sister?

Eileen sighed. *Sometimes family sucks.*

Once inside, she headed straight for Orest André's office and knocked on the door. When it opened, she blurted, "I need to get into the men's locker room."

The elderly man adjusted his eyeglasses. "Pardon me?"

"It's part of my investigation."

"Of course, Ms. Edwards."

As he led her down the hall, Eileen thought about the video clip of Chip Mulligan entering the locker room in the middle of the night. Something seemed off, but she couldn't quite put her finger on it.

"Can you give me a few minutes to clear everyone out?" André asked as they paused in front of the door.

She gave a nod and watched him disappear inside. Minutes later, a line of men—most in their fifties or older—exited the men's locker room. Some of them eyed Eileen with irritation, as though she'd interfered with the National Championships, or something equally as important.

Orest André was the last one out. "All clear."

"I'll be as quick as I can. I just have one last request…"

"You want to get into the lockers."

"Just one. Chip's."

"You got a warrant?"

"It's on its way," she lied. *Better to seek forgiveness from Rick later than waste time waiting for a warrant that might not come.*

André handed her a plastic card. "Locker number four. Swipe the screen and press 911."

Entering the men's locker room, Eileen struggled to breathe through her nose. The stench of body odor lingered in the air, followed by even stronger aromas from various body sprays, colognes and deodorants. Dirty towels had been carelessly dropped on the floor, possibly because of the unexpected evacuation.

These sights and scents reminded her of all the times she'd chatted with Will in the school locker room after a hockey game. She missed those days. She missed Will. Maybe her son would've become the next Wayne Gretsky—or the next Bill Gates. *Maybe…*

Eileen located Mulligan's locker in the far corner. When she swiped the card and entered the code, the door popped open with a soft click. The locker contained a few personal care products, a pair of faded jeans and a stained Barenaked Ladies t-shirt.

No sign of whips, chains or other sexual toys, thank God.

She pushed aside a pair of Nikes. "What have we here?"

Using a pen taken from the pocket of the t-shirt, Eileen leaned closer and poked at something wedged in the back of the locker. A gray club cap slid toward her. Upon closer examination, she discovered a streak of reddish-brown beneath the rim of the cap. *Blood?*

Withdrawing a plastic bag from her jacket, she slipped the cap inside, sealed the bag and stuffed it into her pocket. More and more, it looked as if Mulligan *was* involved in Vivian's kidnapping.

But what's his motive, and who's his accomplice?

She carefully prodded one of the running shoes, flipping it over. No sign of dirt, mud or blood. Nothing on the other shoe, either. The Nikes were squeaky clean. Nothing else in the locker appeared to have any connection to the case.

Time to take the cap to VPD.

If they were lucky, the blood would match Vivian's and Chip Mulligan would be arrested. If they were really lucky, he'd confess and give up the poor woman's location. Then Mulligan would be behind bars, where he belonged.

As she approached the door to the hall, it opened. *Speak of the devil!*

"Find everything you need?" Mulligan asked as he ducked under the doorframe. For the first time, she saw a glimmer of concern in his eyes.

"Yes, thank you. I'm done here."

As she followed him out, he ducked again, and her brows furrowed. "How tall are you, Mr. Mulligan?"

"Six feet, seven inches."

"You have a girlfriend?"

"Nope." He smirked again. "You offering?"

"So, no girlfriend," she said, ignoring his question. "Boyfriend?"

Mulligan shook his head. "I'm not into commitments."

Figures.

"Thank you," she said, handing the keycard to Orest André, who waited in the hall.

"If you ever need golf lessons," Mulligan called out, "give me a call."

Holding back a snide reply, Eileen strode outside, jumped into the front seat of her car, started the engine with a heavy shot of gas and sped away. Mulligan's mocking laughter followed her all the way home.

Chapter Twelve

Larry sat at his desk eating lunch when Eileen arrived at the police station. He slid half a BLT sandwich toward her. "There's tea in the break room."

"Thanks, but I'm all tea'd out." She sat and took a large bite of the sandwich.

"Did your hunch pan out?"

"Why don't you tell me?" She wiped her mouth with the back of one hand and pulled the evidence bag from her pocket with the other. "I think this is blood. Can you get the lab to test it right away?"

"With a helpless victim out there, consider it done." Larry picked up the bag containing the cap. "Where'd you find this?"

"In Chip Mulligan's locker at Eagle Ridge."

"Ah, so Rick was able to get the warrant. Good."

Eileen grimaced and glanced away, but not before Larry saw the glimmer of guilt in her eyes. He cocked his head to one side and gave her his oh-no-you-didn't look. Then he released a heavy sigh. "I'll take it to the lab myself."

"I assume Rick and Cayolla will bring Mulligan in later today."

"Seems like you're assuming a lot," came Larry's quick retort.

With a sheepish grin, she swallowed the last bite of BLT and moved toward the door. "I'm heading home, if you need me."

Eileen stared at the notes she'd taped to the wall in her garage office. Something didn't add up. Mulligan, in particular, wasn't fitting into the puzzle. It was like trying to cram a square peg into a round hole. He almost fit but not quite.

"Need some help, Ma?" Zoe asked, smirking in the doorway.

"Can you play the security video for me again?"

"The entire thing?"

"No, just the part where the guy goes into the locker room. If you can find it."

"*If* I can find it," Zoe muttered dryly. "Of course I can."

While Zoe fiddled with the security footage, Eileen mulled over the catastrophic events at Granville Island. A rider on a motorcycle had come out of nowhere, raced toward Valerie and effortlessly grabbed the duffel bag from the picnic table. Why hadn't she kept walking?

Did Valerie plan this? Is that why she set the bag on the table? Was she involved in the abduction of her own sister?

Eileen had witnessed the devastating results of sibling rivalry before, but this was much more than that—if her suspicions were correct. Everyone she talked to had mentioned Vivian's wild streak. She often needed more money, gambled some of it away, got involved with wrong people and was suckered in to every get-rich-quick scheme. Eileen had an aunt like that.

On the other hand, Valerie was the good child, head of a successful company, and she'd do anything to help her sister. But what if Valerie was tired of dealing with her sister's problems? It couldn't be easy caring for someone so irresponsible, someone who valued money over family. That must have put a dent in their relationship.

"Video's all set to go," Zoe called out.

Reviewing the footage from the hallway of Eagle Ridge Golf & Country Club, Eileen paid special attention to the man in the jacket and cap entering the men's locker room. She replayed it three times before something finally twigged.

She smiled. "Time to call Rick."

She dialed his number, but it went directly to voicemail. She left a brief message, hung up and called Larry. "I really need to speak to Rick."

"He and Cayolla are interviewing Mulligan."

"Chip Mulligan is being framed."

"What makes you say that?"

"Something finally twigged when I watched the security footage a third time." She told Larry about her run-in with the golf instructor in the locker room. "Mulligan is so tall he has to duck under doorways. The guy who entered the locker room on the video is too short, no ducking."

"Someone wants us to believe Mulligan is responsible, and they planted evidence in his locker to lead us to him."

"You got it."

"I'll let Rick know. Where are you headed now?"

"All roads lead back to Eagle Ridge. I'll call you with any news."

Orest André wasn't pleased to see her again. She could tell by the scowl that made his mouth sag and the heavy sigh he greeted her with. "What now, Ms. Edwards?"

"What I'm about to tell you must be kept in confidence," she began. "We believe someone is intentionally trying to discredit Chip Mulligan by framing him for Vivian Winchester's abduction. Whoever this is, they have access to your club. That means they're a member, a guest or an employee."

André released a muffled groan and sank deeper into his chair. "Oh dear…"

"I'm hoping that maybe you've noticed altercations between Mulligan and someone here."

"Honestly, I don't have much contact with Chip. And after the scandal with the Dilworths, we've made it clear to him that he—"

"Wait! Are you saying he was involved with that scandal? Why didn't you mention this before?"

"To be honest, I didn't think it was

important. It had nothing to do with Vivian Winchester. And, because a minor was involved, the court sealed Chip's records. They instructed me not to mention the minor's name in context with the Dilworths." The elderly man removed his eyeglasses and polished them with a black cloth before putting them back on. "Chip was a stupid kid back then. He swore Mrs. Dilworth seduced him. He was only fourteen at the time. Chip's father paid dearly to keep his son's name out of the newspapers."

"Yet you hired him back."

André shrugged. "He's human. Chip made a mistake and paid for it. But he turned his life around, and we've had no complaints in the two years he's been back."

"I'll bet. His last student seemed quite…*impressed*."

"Consenting adults are free to do what they want."

"So, let me get this straight. Chip Mulligan had a brief affair with an older, married woman when he was underage, and he was caught with his pants down— literally."

"Uh…yes, that's correct." He frowned and scratched his bald head. "Come to think of it, if I remember correctly, it was Walt who found them in the shed."

"Walter Winchester?"

"Yeah. He'd hired Chip as his caddy for the day. Chip was late so Walt went looking for the kid."

There's the connection. "Tell me more about the Dilworths."

"Désirée and Peter Dilworth seemed like a happily married couple when they attended our fundraisers." He stood and made his way to a filing cabinet near the window. "I might still have their file."

A minute later, Eileen stared at a photograph of an attractive older man with silver hair and his much younger wife. She had beautiful brown eyes and coppery waves to her shoulders. Her smile held a trace of mystery.

"She's very exotic looking," Eileen said.

"Désirée was from Quebec," André said. "Montreal, I believe. Peter met her there when he went on business. They married a few months later."

"What happened to them after the scandal?"

"Chip's father pressed charges against Désirée, and she went to prison. I heard she committed suicide a few months into her sentence."

"And her husband? Where's he?"

"Peter left Vancouver in disgrace. Pressure from the public and financial hardship wore him down. He had a heart attack shortly after his wife's conviction."

"Did they have children?"

"I…think so. Why don't you ask Chip? He might recall something. If he and Désirée *talked*, that is." The old man's mouth turned down in a scowl.

Eileen stood. "Would you mind if I grabbed a bite to eat in the dining room while I call the detectives in charge of the case?"

"Not at all." André reached into a drawer. "Here's a guest pass." He handed the card to her. "Stay as long as you like."

"Thank you."

André walked her to the doorway. "Do you really think the Winchester woman's kidnapping has something to do with the Dilworth scandal?"

"They're definitely connected. But to what extent, we don't know. Thank you again for your time."

In the Eagle Ridge dining room, Eileen found a quiet table in the far corner. The midafternoon crowd had already cleared out. Only a few stragglers sat at the bar, and none paid any attention to the slightly overweight, mature woman sitting by herself. For that, Eileen was grateful.

She ordered iced tea and a fruit salad. The caffeine would get her mind churning and the salad would comfort her grumbling stomach.

She dialed Rick's cell phone. He picked up after four rings.

"We let Mulligan go," he said. "Larry told me what you found on the video, and I agree. He's too short. Chip Mulligan is not our man."

"No, but he *is* connected to all of this."

She filled him in on the Dilworth scandal and the connection to Mulligan.

"I'll see if I can get into Désirée Dilworth's records," Rick said before hanging up.

Picking at the bowl of seasonal fruit, she set her cell phone on the table and logged in to the guest Internet. Bringing up Google, she typed: *Peter and Désirée Dilworth*. Dozens of newspaper articles about the trial topped the page. As she read the articles, she searched for references to other family members, including children.

One article on the trial painted a vicious picture of a sexually promiscuous woman exploiting an innocent child. Chip Mulligan's name did not appear in any of the reports. His father's hush money had paid off. The trial had gone on for months, delving into the marriage of the Dilworths, the offense with a minor and the fortune her husband had amassed. Walter Winchester had been called as a witness, and his testimony convinced the judge to come down hard on Désirée.

The next article verified Orest André had been correct. Dilworth had suffered a fatal heart attack. He'd paid so much in lawyer fees to defend his wife that he had to declare bankruptcy, and the stress proved too much for the elderly man. His wife's suicide was the final straw. Peter Dilworth died two months after Désirée hung herself in her cell.

Eileen read close to a dozen articles on the power couple before she discovered Peter Dilworth's obituary. One line at the bottom sent excitement racing through her veins.

'Peter Dilworth is survived by his daughter, Marie Bettine Dilworth, and his son, Joseph Pierre Mathieu Dilworth.'

No other information, and no ages of the children.

Eileen searched for the children's names and came up empty. No obit for Désirée, either.

Her cell phone rang. "Hey, Bobbi, what's up?"

"You busy?"

"Not for you, my friend."

Bobbi Hathaway, Eileen's high school BFF, struggled with living on her own for the first time in over thirty-five years. Her husband, Rusty, had gone off to fight wildfires across the province during one of BC's worst summers. He came home every month for a few days, and then off he went again.

"I need a distraction, Eileen." Bobbi's voice sounded faint, as though she'd been crying.

"I think I have the perfect thing."

"You working on a case?"

"Yeah."

Eileen ran the details of Vivian Winchester's abduction by Bobbi, hoping her friend would pick up on something she'd missed. After she told her about the Dilworths and the scandal at Eagle Ridge, she said, "What do *you* think?"

"Feels like you're on to something."

"I know…"

"How old were the kids when their mother was convicted?"

"I have no idea. They could've been toddlers or young adults."

"Then you're looking for children between fifteen and thirty-five years old."

"That's far too broad a range."

"What was the wife's name again?"

"Désirée Dilworth."

"You said she was French-Canadian. She took her husband's last name?"

"They *were* married."

"Many women from Quebec prefer to keep their maiden names. Maybe the obituary made a mistake when they printed the kids' surname."

Eileen mulled this over. "The kids may have taken *her* last name."

"Possibly. What are their names?"

"Marie Bettine Dilworth and Joseph Pierre Mathieu Dilworth.'

"I can tell you one thing. You're most likely looking for children going by their middle names. Traditionally, the first name for a French child is Marie or Joseph, depending on the sex of the child. This is for religious purposes. The second name is usually for a relative."

"Then I should be looking for Bettine

and Pierre or Mathieu?"

"Yeah."

"I owe you, Bobbi."

"If you want to pay me, how about with wine?"

"Wine and movies on Saturday, my place."

"I'll be there. And thanks, Eileen."

"Any time, my friend. Take care." They disconnected.

Sipping iced tea, Eileen pondered the day's revelations. At least one of Peter and Désirée Dilworth's children was out for blood. Maybe both. Revenge for their mother's humiliation, imprisonment and suicide? Retaliation for their father's financial downfall and early demise?

Seems plausible.

The tingling in her gun hand confirmed her suspicions.

She spent the next fifteen minutes searching for variations of the children's names on social networks, but the search went nowhere. Too many possibilities.

"Excuse me," a male voice interrupted.

Eileen glanced up, half-expecting Rick. "Mr. Mulligan, what can I do for you?"

"I wasn't expecting to see you here," he admitted. "I want to thank you."

"For what?"

"I have no idea." Mulligan chuckled. "Constable Martin said I should thank you, so I am. I take it I'm no longer a person of interest in Vivian's disappearance. Whatever you said or did, I'm grateful."

"Did he tell you anything else?"

Mulligan pointed to the chair across from her. "Do you mind?"

She shook her head, and he sat down.

"Constable Martin asked me if I knew anyone with a grudge against me. Ms. Edwards, I don't know why someone is trying to frame me, but I'd like to hire you to find out who that person is."

"There's no need to hire me. I'm already following the leads. Rest assured, when we find out who took Vivian Winchester, we'll know who's framing you." She paused, cocking her head to one side. "Since you're here…maybe you could help me with something."

"Shoot."

"Désirée Dilworth."

His mouth turned down. "Ah, you heard about that. I guess I can't be too surprised. Listen, I was a kid at the time, and she was this gorgeous woman who paid special attention to me—at a time when no one else did."

"*She* seduced you?"

He shrugged. "Perhaps. I've moved on from that. It's not my proudest moment."

"Did Désirée ever talk to you about her marriage or her family?"

"Not really. She did mention her husband couldn't fulfill his marital duties."

"You mean sex?"

"Yeah. The old guy was on Viagra or something."

"Did she ever mention children?"

"As in getting pregnant?" He shuddered visibly. "She was on the pill when we met."

"What about children from her marriage? Did she ever mention their names?"

Mulligan shook his head. "No...I don't recall any—" His eyes flared suddenly. "Hold on. She did once mention someone named Betty or something."

"Bettine?"

"Yeah, that's the name. I asked Désirée who that was, and she said it was none of my business. One time, this Bettine called Désirée's cell phone when we were...together. I picked up her phone by mistake."

"Who was on the other end?"

"A girl. She sounded much younger than your daughter. Maybe seven or eight."

"Did you hear any of their conversation?"

"No."

"Did Désirée ever mention her maiden name?"

Mulligan scratched his grizzled chin. "She did once. It was French. When she told me, I laughed and said it was the same surname as some actor dude from TV. I remember she laughed when I mentioned his name. I don't recall it now. The actor performed in a sitcom years ago that was really popular, about some single people living in an apartment building." He sighed. "I wish I could remember."

"If it comes to you, call me right away." She handed him a business card. "And I'd advise you to keep a low profile over the next few days."

"You think this Bettine will come after me?"

"Maybe. You want my advice? Go home after work, lock your doors and windows, and stay there."

He stood, worried eyes scanning the room. "Thank you. I'll do just that."

After Mulligan left, Eileen did a Google

search for sitcoms involving people in an apartment building. The list was long, especially since she was unsure of the year. *Seinfeld, Sex and the City, Frasier, Friends, The Big Bang Theory*—the list went on. As did the list of actors involved in each of the shows.

Eileen glanced at her watch. *Time to head home.*

That evening, she slumped at the desk in her office and contemplated everything Mulligan had told her. The case had taken a dangerous turn. Personal vendettas were difficult to understand, and vengeance usually took a drastic and often permanent form. Companies had been ruined, families had been destroyed, and lives had been lost—all in the name of revenge. In the end, those who dwelled on petty jealousies and wished ill of others paid the dearest price for their bitterness. Karma was a bitch on steroids.

Death brought out the worst in some people, especially family members. She'd experienced issues with her ex-husband's family over the years, particularly after Will died. Since then, Eileen had made herself a promise not to get caught up in their drama and misconceptions. She'd taken their crap long enough while she was married.

Life's too short for that shit.

Chapter Thirteen

She awoke to the persistent ringing of the phone beside her bed.

"Eileen, you up?" Rick asked when she mumbled a greeting into the receiver.

She yawned loudly and flicked a look at the clock. "I am now. You realize it's not even seven?"

"I pegged you for an early riser. Sorry. Besides, I've got info on the Dilworth kids, but I don't know how helpful it'll be."

"Hold on." Eileen sat up in bed, leaned over and rummaged around in the nightstand. "Okay, I've got a pen." *And an old Shoppers receipt.*

"Mrs. Dilworth's birth records list her as

'Marie Désirée LeBlanc.' Her two children were given her last name at birth, as you suspected. Problem is I can't seem to locate them. Records show they were in foster care for a few years after their parents' deaths. Once they aged out and left foster care, they disappeared."

"What were the kids' ages?"

"Marie Bettine LeBlanc was ten at the time. Her brother, Joseph Pierre Mathieu LeBlanc, was six and a half, a bit younger."

"We're looking for a twenty-five-year-old woman and a twenty-one-year-old man."

"And they could be anywhere, using any name by now."

"I'll see what I can find," she said before hanging up.

She stared at the names she'd written down: *Marie Désirée LeBlanc. Joseph Pierre Mathieu LeBlanc.*

Based on what Bobbi had told her about French names, she focused on the names and possible derivatives. Again, too many choices. Without knowing what either LeBlanc children looked like, Eileen wouldn't be able to identify their social network accounts—if either sibling had any.

What had Chip said about the actor with the same name?

She googled Mathieu LeBlanc. Nothing of note. She tried *Matthew* LeBlanc next, thinking maybe he'd anglicized his name. That's when the actor from *Friends*, whose father was ironically French-Canadian, came up.

Eileen was on the right track now.

Wait a minute! Matt—the golf cart kid with one 'T' in his name!

She jumped to her feet, grabbing her handbag and cell phone. "Zoe? Alfie? I'm heading out again." She wasn't sure if either had heard her, but they knew the drill.

She called the golf club as she climbed into her car. When the receptionist picked up, she said, "This is Eileen Edwards, is Mr. André in? This is an emergency."

"Eagle Ridge—"

"Mr. André, can you tell me if Matt, the young man who looks after the golf carts, is working today?"

"Let me check the schedule…"

A minute later, he said, "No, Matt White is off today. In fact, he's off the next few days. Some family emergency. Is there a problem? Did something happen with one of our carts?"

"I need to ask him a couple of questions. Wait! Did you say Matt *White*?"

"Yeah. Why?"

A sudden rush of adrenaline flooded through Eileen's body. Though her high school French was more than a bit rusty, she knew that "LeBlanc" translated to "the White" in English. Matt White, the young man Zoe had fixed the nametag for, was Mathieu LeBlanc.

Gotcha!

"I'm not at liberty to say more at this time. Please don't say a word to anyone about my phone call today, Mr. Andre. Not even to Matt."

"You can count on me, Ms. Edwards. My lips are sealed."

"Have you met Matt's friends or relatives at the club?"

"No, none I can think of."

"Can you give me his address and phone number?"

Another brief pause and Andre gave her the info. She thanked him and hung up. A quick search on her cell phone gave her directions to Matt White's apartment in Coquitlam.

If Matt White really was Mathieu LeBlanc, then where was his sister, Bettine? Bettine *White*, maybe?

What had Bobbi said about the name?

Eileen frowned.

It would come to her eventually. If Lady Luck was on her side today, she'd not only find Vivian, she'd identify the woman's captors and find the LeBlanc daughter.

Based on the prominent signage in the front, Matt White's apartment had more amenities than Eileen had at the hotel she'd stayed in during last year's PI convention. Indoor/outdoor pool, tennis courts, movie room, gym, and heated underground parking? Not too shabby for a cart boy. Especially if he was the son of Peter and Désirée LeBlanc, who'd left their kids nothing but their names. Even those weren't wanted, apparently.

Eileen circled the block before parking her car across the street, where she could keep an eye on the front entrance. Since Matt had the day off, she didn't want to attempt to enter his apartment.

Where are you, Mr. White? Or should I say, Mr. LeBlanc?

She debated on calling Rick, Cayolla and Larry with the news about Matt, but this time she wanted concrete proof they had the right guy. And until she identified Bettine LeBlanc, she didn't want to risk spooking the kid. Besides, Vivian Winchester was running out of time, and if either LeBlanc sibling felt police pressure, who knew what they'd do to her. Eileen's plan? She'd follow Matt, see where he led her.

The apartment door remained closed, no one in or out. After nearly fifteen minutes of waiting, she climbed out of her car, crossed the street and approached the intercom. She surveyed the list of names until she found M. White. He had a second-floor apartment.

On a hunch, Eileen circled the building until she reached the entrance to the underground parking lot. With a glance over one shoulder, she headed inside. Her instincts revved into high alert as she passed parked vehicles that were dimly lit by a single bulb on the ceiling.

Not very safe!

The stalls were designated for specific apartments, guests or staff. Number 108 sat currently unoccupied, but a puddle of oil indicated a vehicle had been parked there recently. About to turn back, she noticed a sinister hump in the far corner under a low beam.

Too small for a car.

As she approached the object, her pulse raced. It *was* a motorcycle. The one she was looking for? A gray cover protected it from harsh weather and other damage. She plucked back a corner and noted the color. *Yes!* She peeled the cover away and dropped it on the ground. The bike had the word *Bandit* emblazoned on it. Then she saw the Suzuki logo. *Gotcha!*

She called Rick. "Hey, it's me. I've got something you'll want to see."

She told him of her discovery.

"I'm on my way. I'll be about twenty minutes. Are you okay there?"

"Yeah. No sign of Matt White, and the vehicle in his spot is gone."

"Don't touch anything, Eileen. And please wait for me."

Waiting wasn't Eileen's forte. But Rick didn't know that.

She paced beside the Suzuki, wondering if she should cover it up in case Matt returned. *No time!* She heard a vehicle engine rev then quieten. She darted behind a wide concrete post as a navy-blue Dodge Grand Caravan slid into the stall marked 108.

When the driver's door opened, she ducked behind an electric car. Matt White, AKA Joseph Pierre *Mathieu* LeBlanc, stepped out of the vehicle. Dressed in black track pants and a plain gray t-shirt, he rounded the van, grabbed a toolbox from the passenger's seat and made his way to the elevator. When the elevator doors closed, Eileen blew out a slow hiss of breath. She dug around in an inside pocket of her jacket. As a PI, she kept a few tools on her, just in case—including a lock pick.

It took under two minutes, and she was in.

Matt's van had recently been steam cleaned, evidenced by the brush strokes in the fabric of the seats. Not a crumb on the floor, either. Sitting in the driver's seat, she reached over and checked the glovebox. A map of the area and some chewing gum were the only objects inside.

She stared at the dash. The Caravan had a navigation system, but without the key she couldn't view it. She flipped down the visor. A spare vehicle key dropped in her lap— probably for a quick getaway. She started the car, praying Matt wouldn't return any time soon.

Technology had always been her downfall, but with Zoe in the house, Eileen had picked up a trick or two. She skimmed over the navigation buttons. On a hunch she pushed the one marked *Favorites*. Matt had saved his home address and work address. Another address, one that seemed familiar, caught her eye.

"What the heck is Chip Mulligan's home address doing on Matt's navigation?" she mumbled. "And why does this say he just came from Mulligan's house?"

Another address listed also seemed familiar. When she looked it up on her phone, Eileen realized the address led to the Montgomery, Carmo and Singh law offices. Was Matt already hunting for a lawyer, or was he trying to get information on the Winchesters?

Like most people, Eileen had had her fair share of 'light bulb' moments.

This was one of them.

One minute she stared at words on a screen, with no hope of solving the case, and the next she was out of the van and halfway across the parking lot, while puzzle pieces shifted   into   place.

Chapter Fourteen

"What have you got, Madam Eagle Eye?"

Eileen grinned at Rick, who'd arrived in record time. "GPS navigation shows multiple trips to Chip Mulligan's house, and I found the missing Suzuki."

Rick radioed in to Cayolla, his voice brusque and firm. "Pick up the warrants for Matthew White's apartment and vehicles, anything registered to him. He's the golf cart attendant at Eagle Ridge." He listened for a minute then added, "I'll bring White in."

"And his sister," Eileen cut in.

Rick turned to her. "You know who she is?"

"I believe so." She held up a hand. "But I want to be sure, so let me make a quick call."

He nodded, his expression puzzled.

She scrolled through her phone contacts, found the one she wanted and hit the dial button. When an unfamiliar voice answered the phone, she knew her instincts had once again paid off.

"You gonna tell me who she is?" Rick asked.

"I have a feeling you're about to meet her, face to face."

Rick's brow arched. "Okay, I'll play your game. Where to next?"

"Well, aren't you going to arrest Matt?"

"Yes…"

"Then we're going to his apartment."

He reacted swiftly, his muscular body preventing her from moving. "You're not going anywhere except to the station. White might be armed. I'll meet you at VPD."

She opened her mouth to argue, but the look he gave her told her there would be no reasoning with him. She scowled at him. "Fine. Go do your thing."

He watched her exit the parking lot and return to her car. She gave him a wave, started the engine and drove away. As soon as she saw Rick disappear into the apartment building, she pulled a U-turn and veered around the back of the building.

Almost ten minutes passed before the exit door swung open, hinges screeching. Matt White, whose face equally represented his last name, flew down the stairs. He didn't notice the beat-up Honda idling in the alley…or Eileen sitting in it. He ran toward her, and when seconds away, she flung the car door open. Matt hit the slab of metal with a heavy thud and sprawled on the ground.

Rick sprinted toward them, his weapon drawn. "Stay down, White! Don't move!"

"Don't shoot me!" the kid shrieked. "I'm unarmed."

While Rick snapped handcuffs on Matt, Eileen sank into the driver's seat of her car and released a heavy sigh. *One down, one to go.*

"Anyone else in his apartment?" she asked Rick.

"No, just him."

"I believe his sister is on her way here, to meet him."

Rick didn't question her. Instead he watched her for a minute. "I thought I told you to head back to VPD."

She shrugged. "You did."

"And you didn't obey."

This time Eileen raised a brow in his direction. "Obey? Is that what you expected?"

He chuckled. "I probably should know by now not to trust you to do as you're told."

"Probably," she mumbled. "Besides, if I hadn't come around back, Matt might've gotten away." She glared at the kid on the ground.

"Take me to the police station now," Matt pleaded with wide eyes. "I'll tell you what you want to know."

"We'll wait for your sister," Rick said.

"I don't have a sis—" Matt choked back the rest of the sentence. "Wait! Okay, I lied. I *do* have a sister, but she isn't involved in any of this. This is all on me. My idea, my plan, my mess."

Rick sighed. "I'd better read you your rights before you say anything more, Mr. White." He hauled the kid onto his feet and gave him a nudge. "Start walking."

The trio made their way to Rick's unmarked police car. Matt scooted into the back seat, his hands cuffed behind his back.

Rick pulled Eileen aside. "Okay, so who

is this mystery sister?"

Before she could answer, a redheaded woman disembarked from a passing bus and strode toward the front entrance of the apartment building.

Eileen grabbed Rick's arm. "That's her."

When they drew near, the woman turned. She recognized Eileen immediately and froze in her tracks. "Ms. Edwards?"

"Liz...White?"

"Yes?"

Rick flashed his badge, and Liz's face lost all color. She looked from Rick to Eileen and back to Rick. "Are you serious? You're arresting me?"

"And your brother, Matt," Eileen added. She pointed to Rick's car.

Liz's aqua frames couldn't hide the tears in the woman's eyes. "You don't understand..."

"You have the right to remain silent..."

The police station grew unusually quiet when they brought in the Whites. Larry gave Eileen a thumbs-up as she followed Rick and his detainees. Matt and Liz White lawyered up right away. Liz tried contacting Patricia Carmo, but when Carmo heard why the Whites needed her, she declined to represent them.

"Conflict of interest," she told her former receptionist.

Cayolla gave Rick a hard slap on the back. "Good catch, partner."

"You can give the credit to Eileen. That woman's got amazing skills."

Behind him, Eileen blushed.

"How did you figure out that these two were responsible for the abduction and ransom theft?" Rick whispered to her.

She told him about the first time she'd met Matt—or "Mat." Since his birth name was Mathieu, it would be natural for him to drop the other T.

"What about his sister?"

"Well, we knew the sister's birth name and that she now may have the same last name as her brother. She had me stumped for days, though. It wasn't until I checked Matt's GPS and saw the address for the law offices that I began to connect the dots. When I first met Liz, she had a piece of fluff on her—cat fur, I believe. I think you'll discover that ketamine was stolen from her vet's office. She's the right age as well. But most of all, it was her name. Like a friend told me, Bettine is a French derivative of Elizabeth. As are Beth, Betty…and *Liz*."

Cayolla appeared. "Let's get them into interview rooms. We've still got a missing, and possibly injured, woman out there."

"If you let my sister go, I'll tell you," Matt cried out. "But I want a deal for Liz."

"We'll see what we can do for her," Cayolla replied.

Seconds later, Rick and Eileen were back in a police vehicle heading to Chip Mulligan's house, with three police cars and several emergency vehicles also en route.

She called Mulligan's cell phone. "Are you at home?"

"No, I'm at Eagle Ridge. Why?"

She explained the situation.

"That doesn't make sense," Mulligan said. "There's no one else in my home. I swear to you."

"What about other buildings on the property?"

"There's a small shed out back, but I was in there on the weekend for the lawnmower. No Vivian there. Other than that, the backyard is mostly overgrown. I haven't even trimmed the cedar hedges this year. Hold on! The hedges!"

"What about them?"

"The property is bigger than what you see. The cedar hedges line the end of our grass area, but behind that is a forest of trees, a steep cliff and the first shed my father—"

Eileen didn't hear the rest. She'd already hung up. "I know where Vivian's being held."

Chapter Fifteen

Chip Mulligan's neighbor, Gerald Picard, sat on his front porch when they arrived. He gave her a wave as Eileen climbed out of the unmarked police vehicle. "Oh goody, the PI is back…and she brought a bodyguard." He raised a can of beer in her direction. *"À ta santé!"* *To your health.*

"Mr. Picard, have you seen or heard anything unusual coming from the Mulligan residence?"

"Unusual? Nope. Just you."

"You see anyone here in the past twenty-four hours?" Rick asked. "Maybe you saw someone go inside the house or into the backyard?"

Picard cocked his head to one side. "You think I keep track of my neighbors? I don't spy on them, if that's what you—"

"It's important, Mr. Picard," Eileen interrupted. "A woman's life may depend on you."

Picard scratched his unshaved chin. "Well, since *you're* asking, I was up last night with stomach cramps. You know how it is when you get as old as me, you just can't eat what you used to. I was in the kitchen and saw Chip's truck pull up in the driveway. Except he wasn't driving it. Some young kid was. Maybe twenty, clean cut boy."

Matt White.

"Luis is on his way, with back up," Rick said, pulling her aside. "He's worried White may have booby-trapped the yard or shed."

"I doubt Matt's that smart," she said dryly.

They left Picard drinking on his porch and approached the side of the house. A metal gate opened into the backyard. At the far end, a row of cedar hedges established the boundary, innocently obscuring the remainder of the lot from view.

"Through there!" Rick shouted as he sprinted across the grass.

He led her to an overgrown opening in the hedges, possibly where an arbor had once been. She pushed back branches and squeezed through. The rough terrain consisted of low groundcover, rocks and bushes. She twisted her ankle. "Ow! Damn it!"

Rick caught her arm. "You okay?"

"I will be, as long as I don't end up rolling downhill."

Eileen shielded her eyes from the sun with one hand and surveyed the landscape. The left side ended in rock and a steep, deadly drop down a cliff. A verdant forest grew on the right side, and she nearly missed seeing the shed. The faded, weathered wood caused the shed to blend into the nearby trees.

She wanted nothing more than to rush inside, but she knew that hidden dangers might be lurking, so she let Rick take the lead. As they approached, he scoped out the land and remained a few feet ahead of her. He had his gun drawn and at his side. Eileen's gun remained at home, safely tucked away in a locked gun box. It rarely saw the light of day anymore, even though she still carried a permit.

The air around the shed grew still, and

even the birds stopped chirping.

The moment of truth.

Would they find Vivian alive?

A new padlock gleamed on the door to the shed.

Rick aimed his gun. *Bam!* The lock dropped to the ground and the door to the shed squealed as it flew open. A massive dust cloud obscured their vision.

"Stay behind me," Rick said.

Eileen winced. "Smells like an animal crawled in there and died."

As the dust settled, Rick withdrew a flashlight from his belt and swept it over the room. They found her in the far corner. Vivian Winchester sat slumped in a chair, her hands and feet bound and a potato sack covered her head.

"Vivian?" Eileen called out.

No movement.

Oh God! Is she dead?

"Vivian Winchester, I'm with Vancouver Police," Rick said as he moved closer to the woman.

He gently removed the sack from Vivian's head, and Eileen gasped. The woman's skin and hair were filthy, as though she'd literally been dragged through the mud. Open abrasions and scratches covered her hands and face. Vivian had fought back.

Eileen felt for a pulse. "It's faint but there."

The woman moaned, but her eyes remained closed.

"We've got you, Miss Winchester," Rick said. "You're safe now."

Eileen worked at the knots that restrained Vivian's hands, while Rick untied her feet.

"Should we wait for the ambulance, Rick?"

"No, let's get her out of here."

With a small grunt, he hefted Vivian into his arms, and they made their way back through the hedges. Flashing lights greeted them. Paramedics took over, and the next few minutes were absolute chaos. After they strapped Vivian to a gurney and sent her on her way to Vancouver General Hospital, Eileen realized something was off.

"Notice anything unusual about the victim?" she asked Rick.

Confusion spread across his face. "Unusual? What do you mean?"

"Her hair is longer…"

"And dirty. Nothing out of the ordinary, Eileen. She's been here for at least a week."

"She's also missing a large ring on her right hand." When Rick raised a brow, she added, "She has a tan...and a white band on her right middle finger."

"What are you thinking?"

"That there's more to this case. That maybe we missed something." Her eyes flared widely. "We need to go to the hospital. Now!"

Rick stared at her for a second, then headed for the police vehicle. "Let's go then."

"You're not going to ask me why?"

He grinned. "I think you're enjoying the big reveal. Why spoil it?"

On the drive to the hospital, Eileen ran the facts of the case through her mind, focusing on a few inconsistencies. Sure, they had Matt and his sister in custody, but the final piece of the puzzle was missing, and she now knew who held it.

She peeked at Rick, curious why he hadn't pushed her to reveal her thoughts. He was a patient man, unlike her ex-husband.

At Vancouver General, they were directed to a private room.

The victim sat upright in the hospital bed, her face fifty shades of purple and gray, and a thick bandage wrapped around her head. Her eyes were closed.

"Miss Winchester?" Rick began, holding up his badge. "We'd like to ask you a few questions."

The woman opened her eyes, flinched and nodded.

"Can you tell us what happened the day you were abducted?"

"I don't remember everything clearly," she said in a hoarse voice. "It happened so fast. Matt called me to meet in the back woods at Eagle Ridge. He said it was something important to do with my sister. When I got there, he gave me a bottle of iced tea, and we walked in the woods for a while, talking about everything except why he asked me to meet. Finally, I demanded to know what was going on. But I passed out before I heard Matt's reply." She gently massaged her jaw. "I must've hit the ground hard because I lost a tooth in the fall."

"Mr. White drugged you with ketamine he confiscated from a veterinarian."

The woman nodded. "When I woke up, I was in the shed. Sometimes when Matt was there, I pretended to be unconscious, so I'm aware of the part his sister played in this." A tear rolled down one cheek. "I still don't understand why Matt did this to me. For money?"

"I'm pretty sure Matt and his sister weren't the only ones involved," Eileen said.

An astonished Rick caught her gaze. "What?"

Footsteps sounded in the hallway, not far from the armed guard posted outside room. Clickety-clack, clickety-clack.

"I think we're about to meet the person responsible," she said.

Valerie Winchester swept into the room. "Vivian! They found you!"

The woman in the bed blinked. "Vivian? Wait—what did you do to your hair?"

"Oh sweetie, you're still in shock." Valerie swooped down and hugged her. "I'll take care of you. We'll get you the best doctors and psychologists to get you through this, Vivian."

"I don't need a psychologist. And why are you calling me by *your* name?" She turned to Rick and Eileen. "I'm *Valerie* Winchester. She's Vivian."

"Wait a minute." Rick glanced from sister to sister. "What's going on here?"

Eileen smiled. "Isn't it clear, Rick? Our victim is the real Valerie Winchester. We thought we were looking for 'Vivian,' but she's been here all along. Right, Viv?"

The woman standing over the hospital bed swallowed hard. "My sister needs rest. She doesn't know what she's say—"

"Vivian! How could you do this to me? You're my baby sister. I've done everything to protect you. I've always looked after you, *loved* you."

"Loved me?" The real Vivian seethed. "You've controlled me ever since our parents died. You're jealous of my popularity. You judge my every move. And I'm sick to death of having to clear every expense through you. That money is half mine."

"Of course it is!" Valerie cried. "It always has been yours. I was only protecting you from—"

"From who, Valerie? From me?"

The woman in the bed sobbed. "Yes, from you. You're not thinking straight. Look what you've done!"

Rick waved to the guard, who entered the room. "Please take Miss Vivian Winchester into custody."

The guard glanced at the injured woman in the bed.

"The other one," Eileen said.

The guard escorted Vivian out of the

room, leaving a devastated Valerie behind. Eileen felt deeply sorry for the woman. She'd survived being drugged, abducted and beaten, all to discover that the one person she loved most was responsible.

With a quiet apology, Rick and Eileen left Valerie's room and made their way to the elevator.

"How did you know?" Rick asked.

"When you removed the sack, and I saw *blonde* hair, I thought of the salon I saw "Valerie" go to. It was out of the way, not her usual salon. She'd had her hair cut, colored and styled like her sister's. She probably picked up something to help the color last. With their opposite styles and colors, none of us noticed how much the sisters looked alike. And after I noticed the white band on the victim's finger, I thought of the ring her sister was wearing—her father's ring."

"Sibling rivalry…"

"Gone bad in a big way. Greed makes people do terrible things, even to family."

"Good thing we're not rich then, isn't it?" he joked.

"How do you know I'm not? Maybe VPD gave me a stellar payout when I left."

"Did they?"

She blew out a sheepish breath. "No."

Epilogue

When Eileen opened the front door, Larry held out a bottle of Pinot Gris. "We need to celebrate this one."

"You're late. I started without you." She pointed to the half-empty bottle of Arbor Mist on her dining room table. "But I can always use more. You know what they say now. Wine is the new exercise."

"I believe they're referring mainly to *red* wine."

Eileen flung a hand in the air. "Red, white, blush—it's all wine to me."

Larry strode to the cupboard and retrieved a glass.

"What are we toasting to, exactly?" she

asked.

"Your eagle eye, that's what."

"Don't forget Zoe. She's the one who found the clues in the eagle's nest."

"She may not be your daughter by birth, but she sure thinks like you." He draped a fatherly arm across her shoulders. "Without you on this case, we might not have caught the people responsible for Valerie Winchester's abduction, and she'd probably be dead. You always notice the smallest things in people. Thank God for that."

With Vivian Winchester and the Whites—aka the LeBlancs—behind bars, and the real Valerie Winchester overseeing her empire from a hospital bed, the abduction case was officially closed. Vivian admitted to blackmailing the Whites into helping her, not knowing who they really were or that they were using her too. Liz White had stolen the money from the trust. As Patricia Carmo's receptionist, she had access to bank accounts. Vivian had caught Liz in the act and came up with the scheme to kidnap her sister—if the Whites assisted her.

Matt and Liz remained focused on their own revenge plan, while the real Vivian took her sister's place and money. But she remained adamant that she'd never intended to murder her sister. That was all on Matt, she told them later. The idea had been that they'd be paid the three million ransom and would give up any other plans for vengeance. Valerie would be set free but would end up in a psychiatric ward due to identity confusion, complications arising from her injuries. Pinning everything on Chip Mulligan proved to be Vivian's idea, too.

The phone rang.

"Hey, Eileen."

"Rick, what's up?"

"I, uh, was wondering if you'd like to go out for a drink, to celebrate."

"Sure. Who all's going? Larry's here, by the way."

"Oh…yeah…okay, he can come too, if you want…"

Eileen bit her bottom lip. "Wait. Did you mean just *us*? Like…you and me?" *Like a…date?*

"No big deal if you're busy."

Eileen stared up at the ceiling. What was it with men who couldn't say what they meant? "Sure. Where do you want to meet?"

Her eyes met Larry's across the table, and he nodded his approval, stood, downed the last inch of wine and motioned toward the door. With a wave, he disappeared into the dead of night.

"Monty's Pub?" Rick suggested.

Eileen had spent many a night drinking at Monty's, a well-known cop bar a few blocks from the station, especially after Will died. "I know the place. I'll be there in an hour."

After she hung up, she saw Zoe standing a few feet away, her eyes twinkling and a smile stretching from ear to ear. She handed Eileen a folded piece of paper.

"What's this?"

"I figure since you're getting paid, and I helped you solve the case," Zoe said, "I should at least get minimum wage for my hours. This is my invoice. You can pay me by Paypal or e-transfer."

Damn, the kid was too smart. But she had a point.

Eileen examined the invoice. "Fifteen dollars an hour is minimum wage?"

Zoe shrugged. "I added a little extra because I'm fast on a computer. I'm worth it, aren't I?"

Eileen put an arm around the girl's shoulders. "You're worth every penny."

"Maybe I should work for you full-time."

"Hey, don't go getting ideas about ditching school. I had to pull a lot of strings to get you enrolled where you are. Besides, you only have two years before you graduate."

"Can I work for you afterward?"

"Let's just get you graduated first."

Zoe paused in the doorway. "You still owe me a day at the PNE, Ma."

"How about this Saturday?"

Zoe grinned. "Done! Now go get ready for your date."

"It's not a date. It's just drinks with a colleague."

Zoe stared at her for a long moment then said the one word that made most parents cringe, "*Whatever*." With a satisfied grin, she skipped off down the hall.

Eileen flicked an irritated look at her reflection in the mirror. "It's *not* a date!"

~ * ~

If you enjoyed this book, please consider writing a short review and posting it on your favorite review site. Reviews are very helpful to other readers and are greatly appreciated by authors like me.

Drop me an email and I may feature part of your review on my blog/site. Thank you.

cherylktardif@shaw.ca

FOR MY FATHER, LARRY.
I wish you'd read this one! I miss you. R.I.P.
in the multiverse...

Acknowledgements

My sincere thanks to editor M.J. Moores, for all her wisdom and reminders of things forgotten. You've made *EAGLE E.Y.E.* shine!

To Ryan Doan, for creating an awesome cover for this mystery novella, and for always having an "eagle eye" for detail. Thank you!

To my mother, Mary, for giving me feedback on this story when I needed it most, especially when I wasn't sure if I'd "pulled off" the big twist at the end.

Special thanks to Friends Pub owner Juggy Dhaliwal, plus Rachel, Stacy and everyone at Friends Pub in West Kelowna, for your awesome support, enthusiasm and great service (and music!) as I wrote this book in the far back corner of your establishment. Having an inspiring place to write is all part of my process, and I couldn't have done it without you. Thank you!

To my husband, Marc, for always having my back, and for giving me the freedom to pursue my dreams. I love you always.

To the Universe, for giving me the means to fulfill my goals and dreams. I know I am lucky. I am truly grateful for all the wonderful things in my life!

Praise for EAGLE E.Y.E.

"I read this sensational novella in one sitting. It's an intricately-woven plot that was extremely hard to put down. Excellent, intriguing mystery from start to finish." — M.A. Comley, *New York Times* bestselling author of the Justice series

"A captivating mystery, intricately plotted and hard to put down!" —Kim Cresswell, award-winning author of the Whitney Steel Series

Message from the Author

Dear Reader,

Thank you so much for reading my E.Y.E. Spy Mystery series, featuring some of my personal favorite characters: Eileen, Zoe, Larry and Alfie. This is the first work completed *after* the death of my father, Larry Norman Kaye, and the first one he won't get to read. My father will live on through his character "Larry Norman." *This book is for you, Dad...R.I.P.*

While I'm saddened by loss, I am thrilled that YOU, dear reader, have this opportunity. I hope you have enjoyed seeing Eileen open up to her foster daughter, Zoe/Zipper, and vice versa. I am rather fond of these characters. And I'm excited about what will happen next. But I can't tell you. Not yet. ☺

I'm also working on a thriller that may just be my best. It's taking a bit longer than expected, but I want to make sure this story grabs you and doesn't let go.

Drop me an email, or connect with me on Facebook, Twitter, etc. I love hearing from readers.

Happy reading!

~ Cheryl Kaye Tardif

Works by Cheryl Kaye Tardif

Novels:
SUBMERGED
CHILDREN OF THE FOG
WHALE SONG (Includes School Edition with discussion guide for schools/book clubs and Large Print edition)
DIVINE INTERVENTION
DIVINE JUSTICE
DIVINE SANCTUARY
THE RIVER
LANCELOT'S LADY

Novellas/Qwickies:
EAGLE E.Y.E. (Qwickie)
E.Y.E. OF THE SCORPION (Qwickie)
INFESTATION (Qwickie)

Anthologies or Collections:
SKELETONS IN THE CLOSET & OTHER CREEPY STORIES
WHAT FEARS BECOME
SHADOW MASTERS
A FEAST OF FRIGHTS FROM THE HORROR ZINE
25 YEARS IN THE REARVIEW MIRROR: 52 Authors Look Back

Bundles & Trilogies:
DIVINE TRILOGY

Short Stories:
DREAM HOUSE
REMOTE CONTROL

Children's Books:
THE ELFLING PRINCESS

Foreign Translations:
VERSUNKEN (German - Submerged)
LES ENFANTS DU BROUILLARD (French - Children of the Fog)
DIVINE: Blick ins Feuer (German - Divine Intervention)
WILDER FLUSS (German - The River)
DES NEBELS KINDER (German - Children of the Fog)
DIE MELODIE DER WALE (German - Whale Song)
DIE MELODIE DER WALE: Schulausgabe (German - Whale Song: School Edition)
LANCELOTS LADY (German - Lancelot's Lady)
GIZEMLI NEHIR (Turkish - The River)
2 Chinese titles (Out of print – Whale Song and Children of the Fog)

Non-Fiction:
HOW I MADE OVER $42,000 IN 1 MONTH SELLING MY KINDLE eBOOKS

Audio Books:
CHILDREN OF THE FOG
SUBMERGED
DES NEBELS KINDER (German – Children of the Fog)
WHALE SONG

About the Author

Cheryl Kaye Tardif is an award-winning, international bestselling Canadian suspense author. Some of her most popular novels have been translated into foreign languages. She is best known for CHILDREN OF THE FOG, SUBMERGED, THE RIVER, DIVINE TRILOGY and WHALE SONG.

When people ask her what she does, Cheryl likes to say, "I kill people off for a living!" You can imagine the looks she gets. Sometimes she'll add, "Fictitiously, of course. I'm a suspense author." Sometimes she won't say anything else.

Inspired by Stephen King, Dean Koontz and others, Cheryl strives to create stories that feel real, characters you'll love or hate, and a pace that will keep you reading.

In 2014, she penned E.Y.E. OF THE SCORPION,

her first "Qwickie" (novella) for Imajin Books new imprint, Imajin Qwickies. She followed this with INFESTATION, a Qwickie horror novella inspired by true events.

Born in Vancouver, BC, and raised in BC, Alberta and Bermuda, she now resides in West Kelowna, BC. Cheryl is working on her next thriller—one that is sure to plague readers' dreams.

Booklist raves, "Tardif, already a big hit in Canada…a name to reckon with south of the border."

Cheryl's website: www.cherylktardif.com
Blog: www.cherylktardif.blogspot.com
Twitter: www.twitter.com/cherylktardif
Facebook:
https://www.facebook.com/CherylKayeTardif

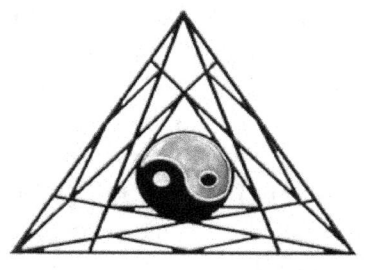

IMAJIN BOOKS[®]
Quality fiction beyond your wildest dreams

For your next eBook or paperback purchase,
please visit:

www.imajinbooks.com

www.imajinbooks.blogspot.com

www.twitter.com/imajinbooks

www.facebook.com/imajinbooks

IMAJIN QWICKIES[®]
www.ImajinQwickies.com